Praise for *This Seat's Saved*

You know the feeling. Like a punch in the gut. You can't breathe. Heather Holleman captures that left-out feeling so well. This story will grab you by the heart.

CHRIS FABRY
Author and host of *Chris Fabry Live* on Moody Radio

After reading this book, you'll want to tramp through the woods in search of red foxes and spring peepers, flop back in a pile of leaves and cry about the difficulties of growing up, and learn how to see your miraculous everyday life through the lens of God's perfect love for you. *This Seat's Saved* is a must-read for every middle school girl—and for every grown woman who still has a "middle school girl" deep inside. I cannot wait to share this transformative story with my four daughters!

LAURA BOOZ
Author of *Expect Something Beautiful: Finding God's Good Gifts in Motherhood* and host of the *Expect Something Beautiful* podcast

Heather Holleman is a truly talented storyteller. In *This Seat's Saved* she wraps her unique gift with a bow and presents it to an age group I love dearly: tweens! They'll be riveted by the plotline, identify with the girl-drama, and then discover they've been learning a powerful truth from God's Word the whole time.

DANNAH GRESH
Bestselling author of *Lies Girls Believe: And The Truth That Sets Them Free* and founder of True Girl

I *love* this book. You will love it; more importantly, your child will love it. There are friendships, old and new, the woods of Pennsylvania, and seventh-grade life imploding like a science experiment gone wrong. And there is God's kind and faithful presence, evident in everything from strong family relationships to the relationship between a red fox and sunset times. *This Seat's Saved* is not only the story of a preteen girl longing to make friends and fit in. Smart, awkward, and totally likeable Elita Brown begins to find meaning and purpose in some unexpected places, including the woods where she is "most herself." Through Elita's authentic and endearing introspection, Heather Holleman draws readers into a young teen's struggles and her discovery of true friends, the miraculous habits of a neighborhood fox, and a Creator who makes all things work together for our good.

AMANDA CLEARY EASTEP
Author of the Tree Street Kids series

This Seat's Saved is one of those sweet novels where a reader gathers gold nuggets of truth along the way and tucks them in their heart where they'll be revisited again and again throughout their lifetime. I wish this was available when I was in middle school.

WENDY DUNHAM
Inspirational artist and author of two middle grade novels: *My Name Is River* and its sequel, *Hope Girl*

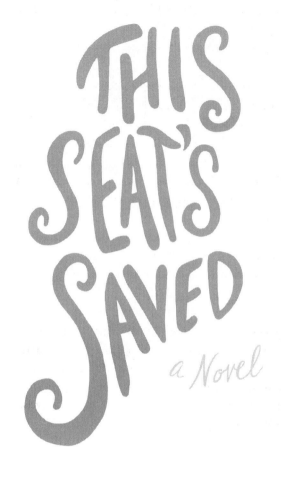

THIS SEAT'S SAVED

a Novel

HEATHER HOLLEMAN

MOODY PUBLISHERS
CHICAGO

Scripture quotations of Ephesians 2:1–3; 2:4–6; 2:10 in chapter 16, Psalm 5:10, and Psalm 30:2, 5 in chapter 22 are taken from the *Holy Bible*, New Living Translation, copyright ©1996, 2004, 2015 by Tyndale House Foundation. Used by permission of Tyndale House Publishers, Carol Stream, Illinois 60188. All rights reserved.

Scripture quotations Ephesians 3 in chapter 24, and Psalm 34:5 in chapter 26 are taken from the Holy Bible, New International Version®, NIV®. Copyright © 1973, 1978, 1984, 2011 by Biblica, Inc.™ Used by permission of Zondervan. All rights reserved worldwide. www.zondervan.com The "NIV" and "New International Version" are trademarks registered in the United States Patent and Trademark Office by Biblica, Inc.™

The quote "All seats provide equal viewing of the universe" in chapter 26 is from the Hayden Planetarium guide. This planetarium is in New York City.

Published in association with Tawny Johnson of Illuminate Literary Agency, www.illuminate literary.com.

Edited by Pamela Joy Pugh
Cover and interior illustrations and design: Kaylee Dunn

Library of Congress Cataloging-in-Publication Data

Names: Holleman, Heather, author.
Title: This seat's saved / Heather Holleman.
Other titles: This seat is saved
Description: Chicago, IL : Moody Publishers, 2023. | Audience: Ages 8-12. | Audience: Grades 4-6. | Summary: Bullied by the most popular girl in school, twelve-year-old Elita's struggle to fit in crescendos when she is accused of a horrible crime, but with her newfound faith, she learns she always has a seat with Jesus.
Identifiers: LCCN 2022052210 (print) | LCCN 2022052211 (ebook) | ISBN 9780802428868 (paperback) | ISBN 9780802475015 (ebook)
Subjects: CYAC: Interpersonal relations--Fiction. | Bullies and bullying--Fiction. | Christian life--Fiction. | Self-actualization--Fiction. | Middle schools--Fiction. | Schools--Fiction. | BISAC: JUVENILE FICTION / Religious / Christian / Values & Virtues | JUVENILE FICTION / Girls & Women | LCGFT: Christian fiction. | Novels.
Classification: LCC PZ7.1.H64625 Th 2023 (print) | LCC PZ7.1.H64625 (ebook) | DDC [Fic]--dc23
LC record available at https://lccn.loc.gov/2022052210
LC ebook record available at https://lccn.loc.gov/2022052211

Printed by: Bethany Press in Bloomington, MN, February 2023

Originally delivered by fleets of horse-drawn wagons, the affordable paperbacks from D. L. Moody's publishing house resourced the church and served everyday people. Now, after more than 125 years of publishing and ministry, Moody Publishers' mission remains the same—even if our delivery systems have changed a bit. For more information on other books (and resources) created from a biblical perspective, go to www.moodypublishers.com or write to:

Moody Publishers
820 N. LaSalle Boulevard
Chicago, IL 60610

1 3 5 7 9 10 8 6 4 2

Printed in the United States of America

CONTENTS

CHAPTER 1

SOMETHING WRONG

I'd never been in big trouble before. Not once. I like to follow the rules. I never imagined starting seventh grade would mean the beginning of the worst time of my life—which included nearly going to jail. I did sense something bad was coming a few days before school started. I knew it as soon as I talked to my best friend, Margo.

I sat in my bedroom that August morning with my one window open so I could hear the eastern bluebirds singing. They seemed jumpy. Maybe a storm was on the way. I heard the oak tree leaves nervously rustling from the wind, and I closed my eyes to listen before I texted Margo. Definitely a storm. I closed my window tight even though I couldn't see dark rainclouds yet. I trust the birds and the leaves.

My room feels like the forest: dark green bedspread, light brown walls, and window curtains dotted with pink cherry blossoms. I keep my stuffed animals arranged like a classroom on my bed, and I rotate who gets to sit facing everyone as the teacher. Yesterday I chose Bunny. Today I chose Huckle the gorilla. I'm twelve years old, and I'm starting to wonder if I'm too old for stuffed animals.

I'm supposed to work on "acting my age" according to my little sister, Cally, who tries to act older for her age than an eight-year-old should now that she's on the competitive dance team. She's the worst. Well, maybe not the *worst*. If I'm being really honest, maybe I'm just jealous. Cally's everything I'm not. She's confident and draws people to her like she's got some gravitational pull. I could hear her downstairs, yammering away about dance practice at the breakfast table over a stack of Dad's pancakes. I ate fast and finished way before her. My mom hates the way I eat. I'm supposed to work on slowing down and not jamming food into my mouth.

I don't talk very much, which my mom says I should also work on. I do like to write in my journal, which is like talking, but it's to myself. It's like my diary, but it's mostly notes about anything cool I learn about nature. Like how birds can predict storms because of changes in air pressure and sounds or how I saw a porcupine in a hemlock tree last week. Did you know they have 30,000 quills?

So basically, I write more than I talk.

I'm also supposed to work on washing my face and keeping my room clean. And wearing deodorant every day. The list keeps growing of all the ways I need to improve. Ugh. Every time my parents talk to me, it feels like a lecture. *Act your age. Eat slower. Talk to people. Wash your face. Clean your room. Wear deodorant.*

I sighed and pulled out my phone. I knew Margo just returned from New York City where she stayed with her cousins for the last two weeks. Before that, she went to an art camp in Boston.

"r u awake? welcome home!"

Instead of a text, my phone rang. Margo likes to call me instead of texting because she talks so fast and is super impatient with how slowly I text. Her voice sounds like how hummingbirds fly. Up and down and lots of energy.

"Margo! Do you want to come over and play?" I blurted out.

"Oh, you mean hang out?" She giggled. I pictured her twirling her long, curly hair. She didn't say it, but I knew what she meant. Play was for little kids. We were soon turning thirteen. We don't play. We *hang*.

"Yeah. You know, go fishing or just walk around the woods or whatever."

"I'm actually busy. I kinda already invited Kee over to make crêpes." She said the word, and it sounded like *crehpa*. A light, fluffy word. A butterfly landing on a buttercup.

"Crêpes?" I asked. But I really wanted to ask why she invited Kee and not me.

"I learned how to make them with my aunt. They're like these little French pancakes that you fill with all sorts of things like fruit or chocolate. Kee visited me on her way home from field hockey camp in New Jersey. We shopped together for school! Eeek!!" she squealed as if she'd been waiting for middle school her whole life.

"Yeah, um, cool." My throat felt tight. My eyes stung. When Margo didn't say another word, I said, "Well, I can't wait to hear about art camp and New York. Did you get new clothes or what?"

"I mean, you could come over, too, if you really *want* to." Her words slowed down now, dark and shadowy. Something wrong. I didn't know what to say.

Before I could answer, Margo rushed into her good news. She never stays in a shadow for long. She's like a blue sky with sun shining every single day. "My TikTok is exploding. I'm doing my outfit of the day and Kee and I did this one dance that my mom totally interrupted and then tried with us. I was dying and so mad, but it ended up being hilarious. Come over. I'll show you the video." Margo knows I'm not allowed to have TikTok. You have to be thirteen, but most kids just lie when they sign up.

"Okay. Maybe I will. My mom and I made brownies. I can bring some." I put down my phone and chewed my knuckle. Why would Margo and Kee hang out without me? And why hadn't I shopped for new clothes for school?

CHAPTER 2

MARGO'S OUTFIT

I ran up the big staircase to Margo's room where she and Kee sprawled out on Margo's enormous purple bed. Margo loves purple *everything*. She's been wearing purple nail polish since like the fourth grade. Margo lives in a big, modern-style house near the university. Her mom is a French professor, and her dad is an engineer who invented something that made them super rich. Margo doesn't brag about it or anything, but she does like to post videos of herself in her house. She posts about fashion, anything involving French culture, and makeup. She calls it GRWM—*Get Ready with Me*—and she shows her followers how she chooses her outfits for school. She started this in sixth grade, and apparently, she's a big deal. Her mom doesn't mind, but my mom won't let me do stuff like that. I'm not allowed on social media until I get to eighth grade. Margo and Kee text me funny videos or links to new songs they like, so it's not like I'm

11

really missing out. People think Margo lives in a mansion because of the big staircase and chandelier and all. And she has her own bathroom right off her bedroom.

She says I shouldn't compare our houses or ever be jealous because my little house is cozy and simple in a good way—like a cottage in a fairy tale. I guess that's cool. She once said nobody has time to get lonely or feel afraid in a small house.

"Elita!" Margo and Kee both cried as they jumped up and ran to hug me.

I took a step back and looked at Margo. Her hair was straightened flat and sleek and long—not frizzy like before. And she had these golden highlights in it. She smiled and fluttered her eyelashes with both hands cupping her face to show off mascara, eyeshadow, and this glossy pink lipstick. We used to play dress up and use her mom's makeup, but this time, Margo meant it for real.

"Wow—you look totally different."

"I had my glow-up. You would know if your mom let you on TikTok," she teased. "Aunt Claire took me shopping for my school wardrobe." She clapped her hands as she ran to her closet. "Here's my first day outfit."

Margo pulled out a purple plaid skirt with a gold belt with two gold Gs and then a black cropped sweater. "They go with my hoop earrings," she said as she pulled back her hair to show me. "And look," she pointed. Shiny black boots that would come up to her knees leaned against the closet wall like they needed to support themselves. She mentioned the brands, and I kept repeating, "Awesome. Wow!" She told me that the Gucci belt was the most expensive thing in her closet but that it wasn't polite to talk about it.

"You are seriously the most beautiful girl in the seventh grade," Kee said and threw herself back on the bed and began tossing a tennis ball so high up into the air it almost hit the ceiling. "What you see *me* in now?" she said as she caught the ball and pointed to her Nike shorts and T-shirt. "That's my first day outfit. This is as good as it gets."

"You don't *need* to look cute," Margo said. "You're an *athlete*, and the boys' soccer team loves you. Who else gets invited to their parties? Not me." Margo kept smoothing out her hair and turning to look at herself in her mirror. "And you have the best skin of us all."

"A party?" I slowly sat down on Margo's bed. Kee's long legs stretched out beside me. She must have grown two feet since I last saw her. She was pure muscle from head to toe.

"Okay, well not exactly a *party*. Just the soccer boys. It was just a bunch of us sitting around and listening to music, and you know, making funny videos. You know, joking about coaches and stuff. And our camps. That kind of thing. And yes, Matt Bouton was there." She glanced at Margo. Her crush. "Stephen Rackley was there. Did you hear he broke his ankle?" Kee elbowed me.

Stephen Rackley was my crush since first grade. I hadn't heard about his ankle. "I hope he's okay." I imagined him on his couch, his black hair matted against his forehead like after he's played soccer.

Margo squealed and clapped again. "You've got to invite me

next time. Kee, you know a party invitation is my seventh grade goal. Maybe I'll have one if my mom lets people come over one night. Music, great food—"

Their voices warbled in my head, drowned out into muffles as my own thoughts took over. A strange, new feeling flooded me; my head started throbbing, and my stomach filled up with the same gross thing that makes you want to get carsick on long driving trips up Siler's Ridge.

A party with boys. New wardrobes. Hoop earrings. Makeup. Shoes. I looked down at my cut-off shorts and T-shirt with turtles on it from the Penn State Environmental Center field trip from last year. I hadn't grown at all, anywhere, in any way. My sandals had dried mud from the creek on them and my shins had bruises from falling off that one log I balance on. While Margo smelled like fancy perfume, I probably smelled like the minnows I caught yesterday for bait. Ugh. Why did I care now?

I caught sight of myself in the full-length mirror. That mirror had always been in Margo's room, but today, it loomed larger, and when I looked at myself, I saw a little girl who looked exactly the same as she looked when she started fourth grade.

I tightened my ponytail. "I left the plate of brownies in the kitchen downstairs. Do you guys want some? They've got caramel in them."

We ate brownies together in Margo's enormous kitchen where everything gleamed, but I couldn't even taste them. And I couldn't focus as they talked about their class schedule and locker combinations and lunchroom plans for the first day of seventh grade, where I was about to hear the worst words I had ever heard in my life.

The eastern bluebirds were right. I heard thunder outside and then the sad, lonely patter of rain on the roof and windows of Margo's enormous house. It matched how I was beginning to feel inside.

CHAPTER 3

THE RULES

The rules aren't written down anywhere, but I knew them as soon as I walked into Siler Middle School for my first day of seventh grade. I told myself it would be just like sixth grade but with harder teachers. I'd go to different classes. I'd get a locker. I'd get to take electives funded by Penn State that most public schools didn't have, like Robotics or Nature Club or even Fashion Design.

I waved and said hello to all the girls from sixth grade I passed by. Most everyone I saw had their phones out, but we weren't allowed to have them in class. You're supposed to keep your phone in your locker if you bring it to school. I left my phone at home. I noticed how people were looking at their phones and then looking up and laughing at some big inside joke. And then I heard them talk about how Margo's TikTok went viral. Someone said, "Margo will get a brand deal. She's verified." Other people took selfies in front of their locker for first day pics probably for their Instagram (which I also wasn't allowed to have). Someone else said, "I snapped you my schedule." I bent down to scratch a mosquito bite and then pretended I was late for something. I had to break away from all the noise in the hallway. That's when I confirmed Rule Number One: Get the Right Phone. And make sure you have Snapchat, TikTok, and Instagram.

Did I have the right phone? Nope. A hand-me-down from my mom so I could text her to pick me up after school on days when I stayed later for Science Club.

My mom's great—don't get me wrong—but she's a second grade teacher, and all teachers think social media kills our brain cells and turns us into zombies or something.

But I guess it's better this way and good for my brain. That's another thing. My mom is always talking about what's *good for your brain*. She cooks fish for dinner because it's *good for your brain*. She enforces "reading hour" because it's *good for your brain*. Annoying. I'm supposed to work on my reading skills. Add it all to the list of improvements I must make. I wouldn't be surprised if my mom *did* have a list of ways to improve me. (PS The Reading Hour, her idea, isn't the worst. I reread *Charlotte's Web* and *The Trumpet of the Swan*, my two favorite books ever.)

Some things about Mom I do like. She's always sitting at the kitchen table and listening to Frank Sinatra. She'll sing along to "Fly Me to the Moon" while cutting out a zillion autumn leaves or little pumpkins from colored paper to decorate her class bulletin boards. She pulls her brown, curly hair up into what she calls a "messy bun" and wears her "cozy clothes" that always involve her leggings and big Penn State sweatshirt. When she's working at the kitchen table, sometimes I help her. Cally wants to help us, but Mom says she's not the best with scissors and glue. She's sort of a tornado when it comes to details. Her room is a mess, for example, and she's always losing things. Half of my life with Cally involves helping find her dance shoes.

I love sitting next to Mom at the kitchen table, especially when there's a pot of spaghetti sauce and meatballs simmering on the stove. My mom makes the best spaghetti with garlic bread. I could live on spaghetti and garlic bread. I also love that she does things like tie-dye T-shirts for every student in her class in case they don't have money for new school clothes. I help her tie-dye every August before school starts. We do orange and black for Halloween and go with red for Valentine's Day. She also keeps a big cupboard of supplies for any kid who cannot afford stuff. My mom can be so cool sometimes.

But back to the rules. My problems started because this *same mother* said no to social media. In eighth grade, my brain can apparently handle it, but not now. I guess my job in seventh grade is to protect my mind. And I'd be busy with all my classes and my elective. The "elective" is basically your fun class.

Which leads me to Rule Number Two: Choose the Right Elective.

I signed up for the wrong elective class. I blame this on my phone situation because Margo and Kee decided on Snapchat to pick the Fashion Design elective. And then they DM'd everyone's Instagram to share the news. So most girls chose that class.

Me? I signed up for Nature Club.

Apparently, not cool.

Nobody told me about how every girl would want to design clothes and jewelry in seventh grade. Except Kee, who doesn't wear jewelry. She's not like that. She's always in workout clothes, but she wears the right brands. But Kee signed up for Fashion Design just to be with Margo and avoid Nature Club or the school newspaper. And, as far as fashion goes, Kee wears everything cool and sporty—the new Nike sneakers and lululemon shorts.

Which leads me to Rule Number Three: Wear the Right Brands. I don't even know what they are—besides Margo's Gucci belt and Kee's Nikes and shorts—and even then, what's cool changes and stuff. Besides, my parents couldn't afford all that. I passed a few girls in the hall who looked like eighth graders, and one had the same belt as Margo. Another girl had on black boots, too. I felt comfortable in my jean shorts and T-shirt, but I guess I looked boring or poor or whatever. Who cares? I don't want to think about this anymore.

CHAPTER 4

THE SCAR

It's hard to explain exactly what I felt on that first day of school when I heard Margo say three words. The worst words. They say that what happens to you in seventh grade stays with you for your whole life, like a little scar, but on the inside of you.

I do have two actual scars on the outside. One on my knee from when I tripped over a fallen log into the stream behind my house when I was seven. I broke my fall on a jagged rock, and it sliced me clean through to the bone. Ten stitches. I like to run my finger across the scar sometimes. I don't know why. It just feels good.

The second scar comes from a moment of pure bliss that ended in what could have been my *actual death*. I climbed the pine tree behind my house last summer. I saw an owl nesting in the tree next to it, and in my mind, if I climbed high enough, I could peer into a nest and see fuzzy baby owlets. Higher and higher I climbed until I could hear the sharp whistle of high wind in the pines. The sap on my hands didn't matter. The setting sun didn't matter. The way the limbs beneath me cracked and broke and slammed down to the earth below didn't matter. I needed to see those owls.

I was in a trance. And I mean like a serious trance. I just couldn't move because I was so filled up with hope about those baby owls. And the sound of it all. My two favorite sounds in the whole world are the hooting of an owl and the way the wind rustles through the trees at night. Both sounds make me feel cozy and hopeful. I don't know why. They just do.

I saw the flash of white and grey owlets popping their heads up from a nest. But then? All I remember is a loud thud of my own body hitting the earth. The tree branch that supported me snapped in half and gouged my right arm as I landed on top of it. I stayed on my back, waiting for my chest to allow me to breathe. The setting sun filtered through the pine trees, all buttery and sparkly. I eventually took a deep breath and realized I had fallen on the softest moss and piles of leaves. And it was like the whole world was washed in gold, and for a moment, I thought I was in heaven. I didn't understand how I was still alive. A miracle? Maybe I started to believe in angels that day. Maybe that's the day I began to believe in things we can't see.

No broken bones. But a stick had impaled itself into my upper arm.

At the hospital, Mom nearly fainted as the doctor numbed my arm and removed the embedded stick. She put her head between her knees and took deep breaths while I watched the whole time.

She's the kind of teacher who can't handle nosebleeds or anything involving blood at all. She says it's the one thing she regrets about becoming a teacher. So I understood as she kept turning away from looking at my arm. Later, she scolded me and asked, "What did you learn, Elita?"

I smiled as I thought of those fuzzy owls and the way the setting sun looked.

I touched the bandage that covered eight stitches. I'd have the best scar.

"I learned that it was worth it, Mom."

My mom took a sharp breath and her jaw seemed to go tight. She was disappointed in me again just like when I eat too fast and forget to make my bed.

But the scar inside?

I walked into the lunchroom. So far, the day had gone well, I guess. The Nature Club email said we'd start right away on an outdoor hike in the woods near the school, so I kept looking forward to that. I had already enjoyed homeroom with Mrs. Crisp who reminded me a little of Snow White with her black hair and bright red lipstick. Mrs. Crisp said everything about seventh grade involved this one piece of advice: *take good notes*. She'd pause and say, "Did you write that down?" Then, I had advanced math with Mr. Rivera, who also made sure we *took good notes.*

I get it! Take good notes!

I don't love math, but my dad certainly does. He's a manager at the hardware store, and he's always talking about whether things are "in the budget" or "not in the budget." Then, I went to third period English with Mrs. Crisp again, which I also didn't love. Again, everything centered on her one rule for all of life on *taking good notes*.

Finally, I made it to my elective class before lunch—Nature Club. I hadn't seen Margo or Kee yet since they had completely different schedules. Margo took French in the morning while my Spanish class was in the afternoon. Kee had English while I had math. And, like we all know by now, they both chose Fashion Design for their elective.

Mr. Dale Robinson taught the Nature Club class, and he let us call him Mr. Dale. Only seven other students signed up for the Nature Club, so I liked that we wouldn't be a big crowd in the woods. When I walked into Mr. Dale's classroom, I held my breath and felt my stomach drop. Stephen Rackley stood there in a blue sweatshirt and Penn State ball cap. He leaned against Mr. Dale's desk, lanky and perfect. His black hair was longer. I noticed he wasn't limping or anything from his broken ankle. I had the strangest feeling inside. I wanted to sit next to him. I couldn't stop looking at him.

I forced myself to look around the room. All boys. Only one other girl. *Okay—good. Another girl. Let's hope we'll be friends.*

Lindsay Myers. She wore a red flannel shirt that she tied around her waist, and she had an old mustard-colored T-shirt underneath. She wore hiking boots. She told Mr. Dale she just moved from Colorado and had spent all summer hiking the Rocky Mountains. Her tangled hair sat in a loose bun on her head, the kind of bun Margo puts her hair into when she wants it out of her face. I walked over to Lindsay and said, "Hey!" but she ignored me and continued to talk about the day she went up

Pikes Peak and how it was the highest summit in the Rockies. On and on she talked. Even Mr. Dale looked bored. He finally held up his hand and waved us all over to him to give us instructions for the first outing. He mentioned bug spray, hats, and sturdy shoes. He told us to watch out for snakes.

Mr. Dale marched us outside the school and across the street where a small trail led into the woods. He told us we'd get right to the work of identifying leaves and wild herbs, so he reached into his backpack and handed each of us our own cream-colored journals that said FIELD NOTES in black letters along with a special drafting pencil for illustrations. I thought of Mrs. Crisp pointing at us back in homeroom about taking good notes. On the first page of our nature notebooks, we found a list of *Endangered Plants of Pennsylvania* with medieval-sounding names like blue monkshood and spiderwort. The next page included the *Pennsylvania Fungi Checklist* of all the mushrooms we could find in the woods.

I loved how I felt inside as I read that list of mushrooms like Witch's Hat and Waxcap and Fairy Fingers; it felt like I was part of something magical, like stepping into a fairy tale. I kept trying to catch up to Lindsay to introduce myself and maybe ask her to sit with me, Margo, and Kee at lunch, but she was up there with Mr. Dale, talking his ear off about mountain goats and swimming in alpine streams in her former life in Colorado.

I walked slowly and noticed the sunlight coming through the needles of the pine trees. I closed my eyes and heard a woodpecker. I stopped and looked around at the ferns, hoping to find the endangered mountain wood fern. I finally bent down and picked a sassafras leaf—I knew it by its mitten shape—and I ripped it in half to smell the root beer smell. "I love that," I said out loud to myself.

"What?" I heard a voice call. Stephen hurried to my side. I hadn't noticed that he'd turned around from the group to walk back to the school.

"Sassafras," I said and held the torn leaf up to my nose. "Here." I then held it to his nose. He pushed his hair out of his brown eyes—same as mine—that looked right at me as he smelled the leaf. He inhaled and smiled at me, his eyes wide and happy.

"That's cool. It's like root beer."

"Yeah." The others were now turning around.

I looked down at Stephen's feet.

"I heard you broke your ankle."

"Who told you?"

"Keanna."

"Kee? Yeah. I'm not playing soccer this year. It was just a sprain, but I'm not playing. Besides, I wanted to try the Math Team."

"Are you joking?" I felt my mouth hang open in disbelief and then quickly closed it. Math? Stephen Rackley was *popular*. He was cute. He was funny. He was part of the soccer crowd. People talked about him. They wondered where he was and wasn't, like when Kee said he was at that party. I couldn't picture him carrying around a calculator and worrying about equations all day long.

"Nah. I like math. Plus, my mom was tired of driving me everywhere for soccer games. Anyway, with my four brothers and sisters, it's not really easy for her. Hey, I gotta run. I'm late." He lightly punched me on the back like I'd seen boys do with their friends. "See you, Elita."

"Late for what?" I tried to ask, but Stephen was already running away from me and headed around the school to an entrance far from the cafeteria. I followed that blue hoodie and Penn State hat until he disappeared into the building. *Where was he going?*

Lost in thought—thinking of endangered plants and how Stephen's eyes looked like cinnamon and the way my name sounded when he said it—I had no idea that my life was about to change forever as I opened the doors to reenter the school.

• • •

It plays in my head in like slow-motion:

I went to my locker to get my lunch sack. I was starving for my peanut butter sandwich and pretzels. I remember thinking of how peanut butter wasn't my favorite, but it holds up well all day. (My real sandwich—my *signature sandwich*—is melted cheese and sliced tomato with fresh dill. I think everyone has a signature sandwich if you bother to ask them. My mom? Turkey on rye with mustard, for example. Dad? Italian sub with extra pickles.) I also packed green grapes and a big thermos of lemonade. And three of the caramel brownies—one for Margo, Kee, and me.

I entered the lunchroom.

I looked for Margo first, but then Kee since she was so tall.

I saw them at the far end of the cafeteria at the high-top circle tables with five chairs each. The fashion elective must have ended early because they already had their trays of food from the lunch line. Margo and Kee sat at a table with two girls I didn't know, but they were all laughing and leaning in toward each other to whisper. Next to their table, the boys on the soccer team kept calling out Kee's name, and then they'd send a few boys over to get Margo's and Kee's attention. I didn't see Stephen anywhere. I lost track of Lindsay, too. I couldn't find *anyone* I knew from elementary school.

I began to walk toward Margo, weaving my way through seated students who scooted in their chairs to make way for me. I called out to her, but she didn't hear me. She was laughing with a girl beside her who also looked like she stepped out of a salon with her perfectly straight hair, hoop earrings, and denim jacket.

Finally, I made it.

I squeezed up to the table to find that there wasn't any room. *Wait, there was one seat left.*

Strangely, nobody acknowledged me. It was as if I were invisible. But then, as I began walking to that one seat, I heard Margo say those words—the worst words. She tossed her perfect hair over her shoulder as she called out to me and shook her head.

"This seat's saved."

I froze. I clutched my lunch sack as everyone stared at me.

This seat's saved. Her words echoed in my ears like the gonging of a bell: *This seat's saved. This seat's saved. This seat's saved.*

"Sorry, Elita!" Margo explained in this sweet voice that made me sick. "I saved this seat for Lindsay Myers. She's from Colorado. Sorry! I wanted to make the new girl feel welcome. We're French conversation partners," Margo said as she put her hand on her chest for emphasis.

Another girl I didn't know grabbed Margo's arm to show her something in her notebook—probably a fashion design from their elective together.

Kee looked away at the boy who kept tapping her shoulder and pretending he didn't. He'd duck down every time she turned around, and they'd both laugh.

I looked around me. What was I supposed to do? The high-top tables on each side of Margo and Kee were filled with athletes on one side and girls from the fashion club on the other.

I turned around and went to the other side of the cafeteria where long rows of metal tables and benches kept all the other students. I finally sat down. The girl beside me didn't look up from reading her book, and across from her, another girl finished a math worksheet. "I'm Elita," I whispered because I couldn't find my voice. It didn't matter. The girl finishing her math worksheet had her AirPods in as she listened to her Spotify playlist. You could have your phones again at lunch, I guess. In fact, the whole table, besides the one girl reading, scrolled through their phones, their eyes blank unless they started laughing at some video only they could see.

My head ached. The sick feeling filled my stomach.

I dumped out my lunch on the table. When I saw the three brownies for Margo, Kee, and me, I quickly asked the girl with the headphones if she wanted one. She didn't hear me. I shoved the brownie over to her and she took one AirPod out. "I'm Elita."

"Audrey," she said.

I fiddled with my watch. 12:30 p.m. Ugh.

CHAPTER 5

THE MISSION

I tried everything to get to those high-top tables.

Tuesday: Lindsay told me in Nature Club that she couldn't wait for Margo's birthday party on Saturday. I already ordered a present for her—like I do every year—but I hadn't heard one thing about a party. When I walked into the lunchroom, I saw everyone talking to Margo. I tried to walk over to those high-top tables, but my feet felt like cement. *Margo hadn't told me about her party*. My eyes filled with tears. I quickly turned around just as the math worksheet girl named Audrey waved her hands and called me over.

"Did you bring those caramel brownies? Do you get the math stuff?" she asked.

I sat down to help her and tried to focus on our math textbook to keep my eyes from darting over to where Margo and Kee were laughing with their new friends at the popular tables.

After school, I went to my room, curled underneath my bed-spread, and closed my eyes. I told my parents I was tired. Cally popped her head into my room to tell me how someone brought cupcakes in for her class and it was Kate who just had a birthday. On and on she talked, and I tried to burrow into my pillow. She said she needed something for Show-and-Tell. I said nothing. She asked if I wanted to play, and I said I couldn't. For the first time ever, she didn't beg me. Maybe I looked too sad. I don't know. I came down for dinner, hardly ate, and then returned to burrow into my bed. At 7:30 that evening, my phone rang. Margo.

"Everybody said yes to my party, and it's so cute because it's a French party. I mean we have these banners with all the French words for party like célébration; festivité; soirée; fête. And it's all French foods. I mean there's macarons, apple tartes, little choco-late croissants—and my cake, oh my cake is totally the Eiffel Tower! Allie Wu's mom made it, so of course I had to invite Allie, right? And my mom said you hadn't RSVP'd yet on the evite, but I know you're coming, right?" Margo took a deep breath. "Right?" she asked again.

"Right," I said. I started to ask about the party and how I never got the invitation. Did I check my email, she wanted to know. Ugh. Maybe it went to my spam. Or maybe Margo just assumed I was coming and was the kind of friend who didn't need an actual invite. I tried to believe it.

"And there's this photo booth where we'll all take pictures in different berets and feather boas and things. Isn't that the cutest thing ever? Do you love it?"

"Love it." I wanted to stop her and ask her about the lunch

table. I wanted to ask if she could please save me a seat. And I wanted to tell her I was confused. Did she still want me as her friend after all? I was willing to be friends with Lindsay, too. But before I could ask her, she burst out something about how the boys may crash her party and how awesome that would be.

"The boys?"

"You know, the *boys*. The soccer boys. I mean Kee is totally with Matt's friend Justin. I mean—"

"*With?* Like dating? Like *together?*" Why hadn't Kee told me? I shook my head and furrowed my eyebrows the way I do when nothing makes sense. *Do people start being boyfriend and girlfriend already? In seventh grade? My mom would give a big "no!" to that. I know there's the Winter Dance in seventh grade, but I thought we'd all go in a group.*

"Oh, wait! I gotta run. My mom's calling me. Bye."

"Okay, bye."

You know that feeling when something slips out of your hands? Like a silver minnow you thought you had in your grasp? Talking to Margo felt like I was watching a beautiful fish swim back into the current. I'd never catch her again, but how could I not at least try?

Wednesday: I walked into the cafeteria, and Matt and Justin were now sitting next to Margo and Kee. Lindsay always raced on ahead of me to grab the last seat at those tables. I turned around and went to the nurse's office. I had a headache, and my stomach wouldn't stop hurting. As I opened the door to the office, I thought I saw a tall boy with black hair slipping into one of the rooms where he quickly closed the door behind him. Stephen? But why?

"Let me take your temperature," the nurse said.

"It's my stomach," I said.

"Cramps?" she asked.

"Yeah," I lied. "Cramps. I have cramps. May I just sit here for a few minutes until the next class?"

Thursday: I rehearsed the whole night about finding Margo and Kee in the morning and asking them to save me a seat at lunch, but I never found them in the hallway. When I arrived at the cafeteria, the popular seats were all taken again.

Friday: I had given up. I felt like giving up on everything, not just the lunchroom problem. That morning, I rolled out of bed late. Who cares anymore? I downed two pieces of bacon, sloshed down some orange juice, and didn't even wipe my mouth. I heard my mom scolding me for my sloppy eating yet again. I threw on a wrinkled T-shirt and pulled my hair into a messy ponytail. Cally, of course, looked perfect in her jeans and new pink blouse. Even though she's a disaster with keeping things neat, she likes to look put together. And she knows not to ever be late since my mom drives her to school. I miss being in the same school as my mom every day like Cally. Dad put his hand up in the air to wave goodbye to them as he sipped his coffee from his chair in the living room. That's where he sits in the morning to read his Bible or check the news. He says he likes to get his thoughts in order before he leaves for the hardware store. He's there every morning at 8:00, so now he drops me off at the middle school at 7:45 on his way to work. I have to ride the bus home, though. In the car that morning, I said nothing. He said nothing. But at the very last second, right before I close the car door when I slip out, he always says, "I love you, Elita!"

That morning felt like I was in a bad dream. Mr. Dale asked if I'd stay in the classroom over lunch period with Stephen Rackley to prepare the trail challenge for Monday. Really? Why me? On the day I forgot to brush my teeth and put on deodorant! On the day I wore my jeans and my T-shirt with an owl on it that said OWL ALWAYS LOVE YOU because it made me laugh last year! On the day I felt ugly and alone and miserable! I had given up all hope of having any seventh grade life at all.

I sat at a desk beside Stephen as Mr. Dale showed us a map of the game lands and how we'd lead the group down to Spring Creek. *Did I smell bad? Was my face still smeared with old orange juice and bacon?*

Mr. Dale explained that Stephen would lead the group, and I'd bring up the rear, and we'd begin scat and print identification. *Oh, why us? Why me? Scat identification! Droppings! Scat is the word for animal droppings! I'm with my crush, and we have to talk about bear and raccoon droppings. Ugh.*

Stephen—with his perfect face and confidence and cinnamon eyes—ripped into his bag of potato chips and, without looking at me and right in the middle of talking to Mr. Dale about bear prints and what raccoon droppings actually look like, reached over and handed me a chip. I took it and ate it. A few seconds later, another chip. Then another and another. I ate like a hungry little bird.

When the bell rang, I snapped to attention and remembered the lunchroom. My weeklong mission failed. *Cut bait. Leave. You're not popular.*

"Elita," Stephen said, "did you hear me?"

"What?" I didn't look up at him. I was ugly and sloppy and defeated.

"I said that I'll see you on Monday. We are the scat experts now!" He laughed and punched my arm. "And don't forget your lunch next time! We need energy for the hike. I can't wait for Monday! Hey, what's your number? I'll text you."

CHAPTER 6

HIDING

When Margo and I were little, we would take our stuffed animals into the woods and set them up in small forts we'd make by the creek. We'd tell stories about how they were orphaned and needed to find food and shelter. We'd collect pinecones and acorns and imagine a feast. We'd tuck our stuffed animals into mossy beds. Bunny and Huckle came everywhere with me.

Margo was glamorous even back then; she'd find some way to turn whatever we collected into an accessory. An acorn wrapped in long grass became a diamond ring on her finger. Oak leaf earrings dangled from her ear. And she'd always tell me I walked too fast for her. "Wait up, Elita! Let me catch up to you!" she'd call. I patiently led her down many hidden forest trails. I pointed out turtles sunning on the logs by Spring Creek and big frogs half buried in mud. She'd stretch out her legs into the cool water and pretend she was a mermaid. I'd have to practically drag her back to my yard when her mother came to pick her up. Her mother scolded me more than once for allowing Margo to become filthy in the woods. Margo's mother had been an actual magazine model when she was younger, so she liked to keep Margo as clean and well-dressed as possible.

After Margo called on Tuesday, I pulled out the box with the French poodle stuffed animal that I ordered online weeks ago. I'd found the fluffiest, most glamorous French poodle. The best part? It was purple, Margo's favorite color of all. I carefully wrapped the poodle in purple tissue paper and wrapped the box in Eiffel Tower wrapping paper with an enormous purple bow. I couldn't wait for her party, even after my terrible first week of school.

*   *   *

I arrived at Margo's house right on time, but many girls already huddled in the house. They were laughing over some TikTok they made about doing hair and makeup before the party. I wasn't invited for that part, I guess. I didn't know two of the girls, but I saw Kee and Lindsay. I heard Lindsay on the phone with her dad telling him when to pick her up *in the morning*. I guess I wasn't invited for the sleepover, either.

I stood against the living room wall with Allie Wu. Like me, she wore jeans, but her top shimmered with golden sequins. At least one other girl here didn't look like a fashion model, but Allie still looked better than I did.

"My mom made me wear this top, and it's itching me like crazy," Allie whispered. "I didn't have time to get a dress when

Margo said to dress glamorous."

"Glamorous? Margo didn't tell me." I pulled at my grey Penn State sweatshirt and felt my face get hot. I looked around me.

The other girls were wearing dresses. Most of them looked like they had their hair done in a salon with curls on top of their heads. Even Kee wore makeup and wobbled around in high heels, but she mostly stayed at the kitchen table texting her new boyfriend for the entire party. The other girls whispered about this and occasionally pointed her way.

I didn't have a word for what I felt, but I knew this: I wanted to hide. My face was burning. I ran into Margo's guest bathroom and locked the door behind me. I looked in the mirror. I looked the opposite of glamorous. I looked normal, I guess. Just me. I smoothed the front of my sweatshirt and thought about the other girls in their beautiful dresses. I had a few dresses at home, but they were too small by now. I didn't understand fashion like Margo. I didn't have a style—except for jeans and sweatshirts that could get muddy or torn in the woods. Should I have a style?

I looked down at my body and then glanced back into the mirror. My eyes looked small and boring. I opened them as wide as I could and wondered what mascara would do for me. I rubbed my lips together. Maybe I just wasn't pretty like Margo. Maybe makeup wouldn't help anyway. I closed my eyes. *I'm ugly. I'm ugly. I'm ugly.*

I couldn't go back out to the party where everyone would be looking at me in my all-wrong clothes. I just wanted to run home, but Margo lived too far away for that. Just as I was about to text my mom to get me, I heard a knock.

"I'm—I'm in here," I squeaked out. "Go away."

"It's Allie," she whispered. "Margo is going to cut her cake and do presents. My mom put raspberry cream in the middle of the cake."

I didn't respond. I couldn't. What would I say? *I cannot open this door because I'm too embarrassed to show my face. And I'm ugly anyway.*

After I didn't say anything and couldn't open the door, Allie whispered slowly, "Elita—look. Nobody cares that you're not dressed up. Everyone is focused on Margo. And the cake is great. And I have to ask you about science. Do we seriously have to compete in the science fair? And are you aware that Stephen Rackley is talking about you?"

"No," I said and cracked the door open. I ignored the part about Stephen, too shy to even ask what he said. "No. We just do a project, but the fair is for the eighth graders." I took a deep breath, opened the door wider, and slid out to follow Allie to the big table with the Eiffel Tower cake as Allie talked about Stephen totally staring at me in class and how he told some kids I was his partner in Nature Club—like he was proud of it and happy. I stayed as far to the corner as I could while Allie asked me if Nature Club was any fun and if Stephen was adding me on all my socials. I told her I don't have any. She stepped back like she was shielding her face from me.

"Whoa. I thought *my* parents were strict."

I took the comment about Stephen being happy to be with me in Nature Club and held it in my mind like a speckled sparrow egg. Precious. Fragile. Too stunning for words.

Finally, Margo twirled into the living room to open her gifts. Her light purple dress was soft and shiny, and Allie whispered, "satin" and gave a knowing nod to me. Margo sat down and arranged her dress around her and smoothed the square neck that led to her long sleeves, each wrist clasped with a pearl.

I stood up taller and smiled. Margo would love my gift. That could make this all better. We'd be right again. I couldn't wait to see Margo's face when she saw the poodle. And my gift towered over the dozens of smaller boxes. I just knew my gift would outshine all the others.

Margo opened box after box of eyeshadow pallets, blush, new earrings, and even more eyeshadow. Each time, she squealed as she explained that finally, being thirteen meant *makeup*. Allie—who clearly spent more money on her gift than anyone—bought Margo real French perfume, and Margo called her mother over to smell it and marvel over it. She sprayed it on her wrists and said, "I feel so glamorous!"

More eyeshadow. A pallet of lip gloss. A silver locket from Kee.

Finally, Margo opened my box.

"Oh. Oh, a stuffed animal. Oh, so cute," she said in a deflated voice. "Thank you, Elita."

She set the poodle down at her feet where it fell over onto its face. I caught Margo's eyes for the only time during the whole party. Her eyes seemed sad for me and *maybe a little sad for her.* I don't know. I can't really explain it. There was just something sad inside of her, and when I saw her sitting there, surrounded by loads of fancy presents and glitzy French-themed tissue paper, I had a split-second moment of clarity that maybe Margo sometimes got tired of everyone wanting her attention. Maybe Margo got tired of always lightening the mood and bringing happiness to all of her followers. The thought immediately escaped my brain.

That's when I heard it.

Lindsay—who wore a jean jacket over her spaghetti-strap dress—whispered, "That's the one Margo told us about. She's such a baby."

She's such a baby.

I looked at my watch. 7:00 p.m.

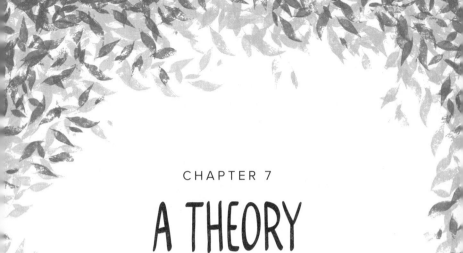

CHAPTER 7

A THEORY

I couldn't face those girls. I couldn't even go near the lunchroom. My stomach hurt every time I thought about eating. And Lindsay? She was just plain mean. I wished she'd fall down in the woods, break her leg, and never be able to hike again. And maybe Margo would post a video that would get her canceled. Margo could use some acne, some bad breath, and anything else to make people not love her so much. And Kee would break up with Justin. Maybe Kee would stop scoring in field hockey and lose all the attention. Never before in my whole life did I hope bad things for someone else. But it felt good now.

I wouldn't go back to that lunchroom. I was changing inside; I could feel it. This new girl, the new me, hated other girls. This girl wanted bad things to happen to other people. This girl wanted revenge. I could feel this new girl growing inside of me as I clenched my teeth and turned away from the lunchroom.

I decided to go to Mr. Dale's room. I followed him into science class where he pulled out his own lunch from his desk. Mr. Dale had a beard and round glasses like my dad. He liked to read the newspaper during his lunch break, but I was welcome to eat lunch in the classroom if I wanted to work on some pages in my Field Notes notebook. He built a special workstation with colored pencils where students could sketch the wildflowers, mushrooms, and leaves from the forest. He also asked if I minded if he listened to his jazz music.

I looked up and saw a big poster with the word HYPOTHESIS written in big blue letters. Underneath, I could see bullet points of a definition. I read that a hypothesis sets out to explain why something has happened or is happening. It's an educated guess that you can then test to see if it's true. Like if you plant three seeds in three different kinds of soil, and one grows and the others don't, you could make an educated guess—your hypothesis—about why the other seeds didn't grow. You'd have to ask the right questions, though. Like did all three seeds get water and sun? What was in the soil that could have made the other seeds not grow?

I stared and stared at the word HYPOTHESIS as Mr. Dale played music from a speaker on his desk. I chewed my lip and thought harder than I had ever thought before.

I wasn't popular. But why? What is popularity? What could I hypothesize to explain what was happening to me? Was it as simple as being a late bloomer? Would everything change if I wore the right clothes, put on makeup, and joined the Fashion Design club? But Lindsay looks like me and she also likes Nature Club. So what's wrong with me? How could I get a seat at those high-top tables? Did I need to know the right people? Am I doomed because I'm not pretty or athletic? Am I pretty? I don't know. Lindsay is pretty—she's got this cool look with messy hair and those flannel shirts. She sometimes puts on lip gloss during science class, and her skin is perfect. I do know I'm not athletic. Kee knew the soccer boys. Maybe that's it. Could Stephen Rackley help me become popular? Where did he go every day at lunchtime, anyway? I don't see him in the lunchroom. Does he eat in a teacher's room? I don't know. But he could help me. Or maybe I could start making TikToks behind my mom's back.

That day, as I listened to jazz music and stared up at that poster, I finished my hypothesis: I would need to reinvent myself to become popular.

🖋 🖋 🖋

The worst part about having a hardware store manager who doesn't make a lot of money for a dad is that he talks about saving money pretty much all the time. There's no such thing as spontaneous spending. We're always checking the budget, forecasting expenses, and seeing how much money we can save. We're not a rich family like Margo or Allie (whose dad is the school superintendent and whose mom owns a catering business), but we're also not poor. Maybe other people think we're poor because we live up on Siler's Ridge. Or maybe they know my dad never went to college. I don't like to think about it, really. It's just another reason to hide from people.

I sat down on the front porch that night beside my dad as he scrolled through the news on his phone. I explained how I really wanted some new school clothes and maybe some makeup, and my dad said this:

"How much allowance have you saved?"

"I'm saving my money for binoculars. I thought clothing could fall under your expense." I pointed at him and raised my eyebrows. "Eh? Yeah? Work with me here, Pops."

He laughed. "How much do you need?"

"Let's see," I said. I pulled out a list. "A skirt, three new shirts, jeans, new boots, earrings. And maybe one of those belts? Oh, and some perfume. And some eyeshadow. I'm turning thirteen. The other parents let their daughters wear makeup at thirteen."

"Your mother and I haven't talked about makeup," he said and frowned. "And I haven't planned for a shopping spree."

"Dad! Come on. Please! You spend a fortune on Cally's dance classes."

"And we bought *you* the fishing pole and waders last summer."

"Ugh. Dad."

"Let me think about it," he said. "Let me crunch the numbers. Let me talk to Mom."

Later that night, my parents came by my bedroom and popped their heads in like little meerkats. They talked about how all I did was come home and go to my room. They asked if I'd joined any more clubs at school or if I wanted to go to church youth group. They asked if I had stopped eating.

"I'm studying. I'm reading. And I eat. You know I eat." I rolled over onto my stomach and smoothed my bedspread out under my palms. I spread out like a starfish, turned my head to the side and added, "And I go to Nature Club every single day. And nobody I know goes to youth group." Our church was small; we went on Sundays, but for the most part, I was bored the whole time.

"You just don't seem very happy," Dad finally said. "You just skulk around and scowl at everyone."

I turned my head back into my pillow and wondered how long I could hold my breath until I passed out. *Would I suffocate in this pillow? Why does my pillow smell like licorice? What is licorice?*

My mind jumps to things sometimes. It's like thoughts bounce the way you skip rocks on the still, wide part of Spring Creek. And a thought is like that first skip that ripples out and out and out.

Mom—with all her annoying positivity—chirped in. "Well, I have good news! Great news, actually."

"Yeah?" I rolled over and curled my limbs back to my body like a sea anemone folding itself in. I propped myself up on my elbows. I do like having a positive mom, I guess. She's like a boat cutting through stagnant water that changes the surface with her energy and good mood. Her second graders loved her.

"I found a job for you. An after-school job—just two hours after school and four hours on Saturday."

"That doesn't sound like great news."

"And they want to pay you each week. Then you can buy the clothes you want, and you can get moving so you're not just flopping around like a dying fish on your bed all afternoon."

"Please tell me it's not babysitting. I have enough of that playing with Cally. Please—no babysitting. I don't like little kids, Mom. And please not sweeping the floors at the hardware store."

"It's not babysitting. It's not the store."

"What is it then?" Now I sat up. I thought of my hypothesis and how I'd reinvent myself if I had more money. Even a little bit of cash would let me get started on the new me. And if I worked hard enough, I could get the new iPhone.

"Can you keep an open mind before you say no? Can you try to imagine it first?"

"Just tell me."

"You know Mr. and Mrs. Burgley from church? Remember how kind they are?"

"And old," I said.

"Okay, maybe. Well, as you know, they live just a half mile from here—when you cut through the woods along the creek."

"Yeah, in the house that looks haunted." Sometimes I'm negative just to balance things out. Mom was beaming with excitement, and it got on my nerves.

"They've asked if you'd be interested in helping them prepare their property to sell their house in November. They need a helper to rake leaves, pull weeds, drag branches to the woods—things like that. And next month when it's too cold outside, Mrs. Burgley needs help sorting and donating things from the house."

"Why me? Can't they hire adults for that?"

"I ran into them at the grocery store. They told me about selling the house, and then they asked about you. And we live so close to them, and they're private people. I don't think Mrs. Burgley wants just anyone in her house. She considers us her trusted neighbors. You know your dad and I have checked in on them for years. And remember when they had the flu and we brought them all that soup?"

"Why are they moving?"

"Warmer weather. Closer to their grandchildren in Charleston."

My mom paused while Dad added this key piece of information:

"You'll make one hundred dollars a week." He smiled and folded his arms across his chest. "You do the math, Elita. Eight weeks." He pointed at me and raised his eyebrows.

"I'll do it!" I cried out and started clapping just like Margo would. Besides, I actually liked the Burgleys. They were quiet but they were sweet. They were the kind of people who bought Christmas presents for families who needed help with expenses over the holidays. They attended high school football games and concerts even though all their children were grown and had moved away. I liked that they lived on the other side of the woods and that I'd get to walk along the creek each afternoon to their house. And the best part? They had two golden retrievers, and I've always wanted a dog. But Cally is allergic, so we can't have one.

My mom was right. I had become a flopping, dying fish. I needed to get back in the water.

CHAPTER 8

SOMETHING NEW

I think I'm most myself when I'm in the woods. Nature doesn't expect anything from you or judge you or anything. It doesn't reward you for being pretty or funny or popular. It doesn't care about your clothing. I could swing my arms in big circles as I stomp around in the woods to scatter any birds if I want. I could hang from a tree limb like a little kid, pretend I was an explorer seeing land for the first time, or act like an abandoned child being raised by fairies and gnomes who delivered wild berries on plates made of bark and oak leaves to keep me alive.

And the Pennsylvania woods, especially in mid-September and October, make you feel like you're in a painting. It's a lot of reds and golds and bright yellow leaves, and it smells earthy and warm. It smells smoky, too, because of all the wood-burning stoves from families nearby who heat their homes that way as the nights get colder. Everything crunches under your sneakers. In

October, deer bound around everywhere at dusk. You can hear them if you're quiet. You'll also hear the wind in the trees and the sound of the creek—just like little sleigh bells—as the water rushes around the rocks and fallen logs. Sometimes you'll hear the shriek of a hawk circling high over your head. Rare things happen; you see a pheasant or even a gobbler and you feel, I don't know, chosen. Even though I know it's just folklore, I still look for gnomes whenever I see their mushroom homes.

I don't know. I'm just happy here. My heart feels warmed up in the forest.

I stayed to the trail. You don't want to get too close to the game lands boundary when it's small game season like this. Sometimes I'd see hunters in their bright orange vests and hunting camouflage, and we'd nod to each other. Most people know me, or at least they know my family. And as long as I stick close to the house or on familiar hiking trails, I can go out into the woods alone. In November, the same hunters come for archery and muzzleloader season for black bear and even elk. I've lived here all my life and I've never seen elk in these woods. Of course, you'll see bear lumbering around, and then, you keep your distance. Dad taught me to always make myself larger if I encounter a bear.

Tuesday afternoon, I walked the half mile down the marked path to the Burgley house. In that time, I started to think about Margo again. *Why didn't she like me anymore?* I walked on, crunching leaves and acorns and stomping out my anger. *Why would anyone like me?* I thought of the hypothesis poster. *Are popular girls confident? Funny?* Stomp. Stomp. Stomp. I was none of those things, either. Who was I, anyway? Back when I led

Margo through the woods, I knew who I was. But I didn't know anymore. And nothing felt right inside of me at school. I didn't want to be a late bloomer. I really didn't want to be me anymore at all. Who (stomp) am (stomp) I (stomp)? I screamed the question out to the top of the pine trees.

Eventually, the Burgley house came into view. It looked gnarled and overgrown, like something out of a horror movie. Just as I remembered it. As I pushed back the forest brush to make my way up to the house, it felt like I was stepping into a new dimension or something.

I stepped through the pine branches and into the afternoon light shining on the Burgley property. I saw leaves and branches for yards and yards. I put my hands on my hips and surveyed the work ahead.

I guess one thing you need to know about me is that I like work. I know it's weird, but I like *hard* work—the kind where you sweat. I'd haul logs to make our log pile for winter and love the way it felt to make my muscles burn from all the lifting. I loved seeing the progress of finishing a job. My mom says my hard work—especially gardening work—is my best quality.

But this house? This went beyond regular work. I looked at all the debris and leaves and fallen limbs and the snarl of vines suffocating the back porch.

I approached the house and paused, my palms hot and sticky. Ugh.

I don't talk to people easily like my little sister Cally does. She's talkative and sometimes too loud. She's the one everyone gathers around. She takes ballet and just started lyrical dancing, and so far, third grade has been one big party for her. What I like about Cally is that I can push her in front of me when adults are around, and she'll do all the talking. I wished she were with me now as I walked up the back steps of the Burgley house.

"Elita Brown! Hello! Hello! Hello!" Mrs. Burgley called out. I thought of how a red fox will cry out three times when he wants to say hello. She and Mr. Burgley appeared from around the house in matching blue and white jogging suits. How confident do you have to be to wear matching blue and white jogging suits? Penn State fans. They probably had season tickets and tailgated every weekend. They looked cozy, like you'd want to snuggle them. Before I could say anything, their two golden retrievers bounded from the house and up to me, practically knocking me over. The dogs had blue bandanas around their necks that made me smile. I love it when people put accessories on their dogs.

"Bo and Bee, sit! Sit!" Mrs. Burgley commanded. They sat and panted excitedly.

Mr. Burgley pointed to the rake leaning against the porch. A pair of dark green gardening gloves sat on the railing. "You can rake everything into a big pile at the property line down by that row of pine. Just make a big pile of leaves, sticks, weeds, all of it. We have so much to do." He was a no-nonsense kind of man. His stern look and raspy voice didn't quite match the image of the cozy jogging suit, and the contrast made me smile.

"Irvin," Mrs. Burgley said sharply, "we haven't even welcomed her properly yet." She squinted at me and reached out a wrinkled hand with blue veins like little streams covering it.

I reached out and gently grabbed her hand, and she swung it

back and forth a few times. "Elita Brown. You are stunning. You are absolutely stunning. You look more like your father than your mother."

I looked down at my jeans and T-shirt. She couldn't mean it. But then I looked up into Mrs. Burgley's eyes. They were loving and bright and sort of, I don't know, sparkly—like something magical. I suddenly pictured Cinderella with her fairy god-mother. It felt like the air itself started to sparkle.

"Thank you for hiring me. I like garden work," I said, still sensing the air around Mrs. Burgley sparkle.

"I deeply respect that. I know that about you. You like hard work. Now—let's get to it. I'll send you home at 5:30 so you're home well before dinner—and your mom's making spaghetti tonight. Your favorite?"

Yes, but how did she know?

Every day after school that week, I threw my bookbag down, grabbed an apple, and hiked through the woods to the Burgley house. Some days, nobody was even there. The Burgleys might be at a doctor appointment or grocery shopping together in their matching outfits. I'd see my garden gloves and rake in the yard, and I'd pick up where I left off. The best part was when Bo and Bee came into the yard. They'd sometimes knock me into the pile of leaves I had just raked.

I'd lie inside the pile and close my eyes, just smelling the leaves. The dogs' tails would thump on the earth, and then I'd feel their hot breath over my face as they worried over me. Lying there, petting that soft, long fur, I'd let the memories ooze out of my brain. I'd think about how I sat in Mr. Dale's room for lunch on the day I looked so ugly. Then the sick feeling: the one at Margo's house and the one in the lunchroom. Then the image and the sounds burned deeper into my mind—the scar deep and permanent. I saw that popular lunch table and heard Margo's words: *This seat's saved.*

Lying in that leaf pile, I felt my cheek dampen with tears. Nothing was going right for me. And just yesterday I saw Lindsay and Stephen laughing together about something. The sun's golden rays filtered through the trees, and as 5:00 neared, right on time, Mrs. Burgley appeared in the backyard with a tray of something sweet and warm. Every day, a different snack. Cider. Hot cocoa. Ginger tea. And always with cookies. Mrs. Burgley firmly believed in snack time.

Mostly, Mrs. Burgley left me alone. She'd watch me sometimes and offer simple directions to trim those bushes or pull up those shrubs. But really, the task was always raking. And these were leaves from seasons past. The fresh autumn leaves would begin falling in a few weeks, and then, I'd rake every day till mid-October.

When you rake old, wet leaves, you're going to find things squirming underneath like worms and sometimes a frog or two—maybe a snake. But the dry leaves and branches of pine I'd trimmed made for the coziest resting place if I needed to catch my breath. Sometimes, I'd run and jump right into a fresh pile of leaves, so I sank down, completely covered.

In that pile, I tried to work out a solution. I could march over to those high-top tables and proclaim, "This is my seat!" And I'd compliment the girls on their outfits and pass out cupcakes or something. And they'd all gather around me and like me and want me. Or maybe one day soon I'd be in some kind of accident and an ambulance would rush me to the hospital. Everyone in school would visit me. They'd say, "When you get better, Elita, you are definitely sitting with us." *Do other kids imagine hospital bed scenarios where your schoolmates all come to give you attention? Do other kids, in other schools, have a mission to find a seat at the popular table?*

One day when I finally sat up and brushed all the leaves from my back and began picking leaves from my hair, I heard Mr. Burgley laugh from the porch. "What in the world is she doing in that pile of leaves there?" And Mrs. Burgley spoke softly but I heard anyway. "Leave her alone, Irvin. She's just working something out."

As I placed my rake and gloves on the porch and waved good-bye, I felt a warmth in my heart as I looked at that old couple sipping tea from steaming mugs. Bo and Bee sat at their feet like little blobs of caramel. One day, maybe I'd get married and have two caramel dogs and live in a big house in the woods just like the Burgleys. I could marry a boy like Stephen.

I walked home, chilled and sweaty at the same time. The work had felt good, *good for my brain*, as my mom would say. I could tell her I felt happy today.

I plodded homeward, but I took my time. Then, like a storm cloud, my mood changed from the happy, hopeful feeling at the Burgleys. I just didn't feel right. I recalled Lindsay laughing with Stephen and Margo surrounded by all her popular new friends. I didn't feel like myself inside. I couldn't shake the idea that I could be someone different, better, *popular*. Did anyone even like me? Do I even like me? Not with Margo around who reminded me I was ugly and unfashionable and told Lindsay I was a baby. And I thought of dependable Kee who forgot I existed. She was lucky—tall and talented and already dating and probably holding hands and maybe kissing. I even thought of Allie who seemed to know exactly who she was. I mean we called her Bulldog Allie in the fourth grade because she was always standing up for herself and others. She'd adjust her glasses, plant her feet, cross her arms, and say, "Stop it. This is inappropriate behavior." She was smart. She was class president in sixth grade. She would be valedictorian someday. Maybe if my father were a school superintendent with a fancy college degree, I would have that kind of drive. And maybe if my mom was a businesswoman who owned a catering business and bakery, I would be a different person and be more like Allie. But I didn't. I was just—what's the word for it? *Mediocre. Average. Boring.* It's like there were these imaginary tables in my head as I pictured the lunchroom. Could I ever belong at any of those tables and take my seat there?

The popular table? Nope. This seat's saved. She's a baby.

The athletic table? Nope. No coordination. Slow as molasses.

The smart table with the kids already in algebra? Nope. I'm in the advanced class, but I'm not the best at math like everyone else.

The music kids? Nope. Can't sing. Can't read music.

Where would I sit? Where's the table for the awkward twelve-year-old who hasn't grown up at all? For the girl who likes catching frogs and climbing trees? For the girl who loves spaghetti, tie-dye T-shirts, and garden work?

I didn't even have a nickname, that's how boring I was. Even Bulldog Allie had a nickname. Margo and Kee had their nicknames. The boys called Stephen Rackley just "Rackley." Maybe one day I'd be cool enough, and loved enough, to have a nickname.

My house came into view, and I sighed. After dinner, I'd finish my math homework and do my grammar worksheet for Mrs. Crisp. She would check our notes from the class before, and I heard her voice in my head saying, "Whatever you do and wherever you are, take good notes."

Maybe I'd play school with my stuffed animals before bedtime. Deep inside, I guess I *was* still a baby. Ugh.

Then something happened. Something that would change everything.

CHAPTER 9

CURIOUS QUESTIONS

I froze and crouched down. I heard the snap of a twig and the shaking of fern leaves. Then I saw it. A flash of red and white. I moved off the trail and hid behind a tree. Something was there. I crept down, still as a stone. I held my breath as I peered toward the sound. I'm good at making myself small and quiet.

A beautiful red fox—long and sleek—trotted peacefully across the edge of the woods in my backyard. He was red and silver with a white chest, shiny black nose, and black-tipped ears. He passed through my backyard and then picked up the trail in the woods that led to the creek and then eventually to a meadow. I stepped out from behind the tree to see him one more time, and the noise startled him. His pointed red ears turned. He stopped and looked over his shoulder at me, evaluating me somehow, tilting his nose up and down. Then he went back to his secret work. The air around him seemed to sparkle like at Mrs. Burgley's house. When the fox disappeared into the ferns, I imagined I saw plumes of fairy dust like if we were in a cartoon. Sometimes I add in details to a scene that I *want* to be true, even if it's just make-believe.

I looked at my watch. 6:07 on Tuesday evening.

On Wednesday night, I walked home from the Burgleys after two hours of pulling dead branches and summer plants from their garden beds. The air was colder now, so I walked quickly. The same thing happened with my bad mood. First, I was happy at the Burgleys, and then, as I left, a dark cloud came over my heart.

Then I remembered that fox. I looked at my watch and stopped. 6:05 p.m. I looked into the woods to my right, and then I looked into the distance on my left. I hid behind a tree and crouched down. I slowed my breathing and inched back into the ferns to hide. Then, right at 6:07, that fox came happily trotting along the edge of my backyard. *Same time. Same path. Same fox.*

I ran home, climbed the stairs to my bedroom, and pulled out my Field Notes journal. I wrote this:

Two nights in a row. 6:07. Forest edge. Heading west into the sunset to creek or meadow. Maybe a hunting trail? Questions:

1. Can foxes tell time?

2. Do foxes have a hunting path?

On Thursday, it rained so hard after school that Mrs. Burgley called to cancel my work. They weren't ready for any inside housework yet, so I'd just stay home. I didn't mind because when it rains, my mom gets in what she calls her *cozy mood*. She lights candles. She makes hot cocoa. She plays Frank Sinatra music and announces she wants to roast things. And as September neared its end, my mom always filled the kitchen with apple turnovers and cider from the fruit farm down the road. Every year, she starts decorating for fall in September. And I mean decorating like crazy. She brings out four boxes of decorations: pumpkins, gourds, garlands of autumn leaves, orange lights for the windows. I love how the whole house smells like cinnamon and pumpkin by the time she's finished.

I sat in my room by the window looking over the backyard. I could smell roasted chicken and the butternut squash and garlic. I heard the garage door open and Dad holler out a hearty "Hello." Cally's voice followed as she told Mom *everything* about her dance class. Sometimes when I'm in my room and I hear the family downstairs and smell dinner cooking, I get this feeling of happiness and safety. Maybe I'm like my mom, and I get into cozy moods, too.

At 6:05, I went down to the back porch where my parents loved to sit at night and sometimes in the mornings, too. We also have a porch swing where Cally and I sit in the summer to eat popsicles and ice cream sandwiches.

"Watching the rain?" my dad said as he came out to the porch.
"Yeah."

We stood there in silence, and then Dad whispered, "Do you see that red fox? He's on some hunting path. I've seen him this same time so many times." He looked at his watch. "6:07," he reported.

"I've seen him. I've seen him three times now."

I looked out and saw that happy trotting fox. The rain didn't change his schedule.

"Dad, he's bigger than I thought foxes are."

"I think he's the male. But I can't be sure. His face seems broader."

"Is he hunting?"

"Yes. And he's smart. See how he's just following the tree line and then going down to the creek? He's figured out how to avoid trapping. Hunters won't lay traps on private property."

"*What* is he hunting?" I whispered in case the fox could still hear me.

"Mice most likely. Rabbits. Crickets. He's headed to that meadow. See how he'll hide himself from view in the understory and go into those ferns?"

"The understory? What's the understory?" I asked quietly. But we didn't have to whisper anymore.

"That's what you call the layer of plants beneath the canopy of trees overhead. All those plants growing in low light keep everything humid and warm—that's why you get all the moss, fern, fungi. You know. All that stuff. You should ask Mr. Dale about it in that Nature Club."

"I will!" I called out over my shoulder as I turned and ran into the house and back up the stairs. My mom called out that dinner was ready, but I had to do something first. I wanted to *take good notes*. All I could think about was that fox. I wasn't in a bad mood; I wasn't worried about Margo; I wasn't thinking about Stephen. Something deeper than my good or bad mood or worries or even thoughts was happening to me. My whole brain was filled up with curiosity.

I opened my Field Notes notebook and wrote my list of observations:

Thursday: *Weather does not affect the hunting schedule. 6:07 p.m. Fox trots down the trail. Vocabulary List: 1. understory. Question: How is the fox telling time?*

I wrote something else but then erased it furiously. I wrote, "Is the fox magical?" I remembered the sparkling of fairy dust I imagined in the setting sun. Fairy tales were for babies, right? I wasn't a baby.

CHAPTER 10

THE BEST DAY

For the first time since school started three weeks ago, I woke up excited to get there. I couldn't wait to tell Mr. Dale about my fox and my hypothesis that foxes *tell time* and that they are so scheduled that weather doesn't change their course.

In Nature Club, I ran up to Mr. Dale's desk. Stephen lifted his head from where he was coloring something in his Field Notes journal, leaned back in his seat, and smiled as he watched me. I didn't have time to smile back. But I didn't mind that Stephen was watching me. Today I felt great. I felt beautiful even. I had my hair in two braids, and I was wearing my best jeans with a buttercup yellow blouse that I sometimes wore to church. That morning, I put on the lip gloss my mom put in my Christmas stocking last year. It tasted like lemon, my favorite flavor.

I spread open my Field Notes journal where I tried to sketch a picture of my fox. I said, "The same time. He comes at the same time."

"Whoa—catch your breath, Elita. Who comes? Where?" Mr. Dale looked down at my journal. I was talking so fast and using my hands to emphasize every point I made—the fox, the weather, the timing. I then told him about the *understory*.

"Elita Brown, you are a naturalist!" Mr. Dale exclaimed with shining eyes. He slapped his hand down on the desk and said, "This is just superb."

"What's a naturalist?" I said, finally calming down as I closed my journal. By this time, Stephen had joined us and was looking over my shoulder. He smelled like the woods and a little like soap.

"A true student of nature. Someone who is becoming a wildlife expert."

"Me?" I said.

"If you're here during lunch again today, you can plan a hypothesis about this fox and his travel schedule. How can you test whether a fox can tell time? What allows him to tell time?"

My cheeks burned red, but not with embarrassment. Not the red-hot burn of shame in Margo's guest bathroom or when I heard Lindsay Myers say I was a baby. This red? I was excited and proud of myself. Stephen smiled and watched us. Then he went back to his own journal, still smiling.

As Mr. Dale played jazz during lunch, he called out over his desk to me. "Elita, you are way ahead of everyone else in our science project assignment. If you watch for that fox each night, you'll have so much data already collected. In fact, hold on—"

He scooted away from his desk and began shuffling through

his cabinets. He came over to me and unrolled a big sheet of graph paper.

"Do you know what it means to draw something *to scale*?"

I shook my head. "I bet my dad could help me."

"To scale means that you'd draw a miniature version of your backyard on this paper. You'd measure your backyard, for example. If it's thirty feet across, you scale it down to three feet across on this paper. And you could put landmarks of where the trees are and your house. You could draw where that trail is, and the creek and the meadow. And each night you'd track the trail and the time."

"Yeah. I understand. Can my dad still help me measure?" I wanted to start hopping up and down. At that moment, I felt for the first time that maybe I *did* know who I was. I was a *naturalist*. I would add that to my vocabulary list.

"Certainly. And Elita?"

"Yeah?"

"I think you'll want to start watching if your fox comes a little earlier each night now that it's late September."

"Why?" I said.

"I want *you* to think about it. This is my own hypothesis I'll test about your fox."

When lunch ended and students streamed in for science class, I went to my seat. Mr. Dale began class by talking about how something really exciting had happened that he couldn't wait to talk about. I sat there waiting for his news. I thought he might mention something new in the game lands or some sighting of a bear or elk.

"It's something Elita Brown brought to my attention today."

I smiled. I tilted my chin up a little in the air. I couldn't help it.

"She designed a terrific hypothesis based on an observed phenomenon. It involves a red fox that I'll let Elita tell you about now. But next week, we'll all present our observed phenomenon to the class. Elita?"

I stood up and turned to the class. I was too excited to be nervous. I blurted out how I had seen the beautiful red fox walk along the exact same hunting path at the exact same time for several nights. I explained how I wanted to see if foxes tell time and if anything could alter the course of his travels, whether obstacles or weather or something. "And it's important," I said, but I hadn't really thought about that part yet. "It's important because . . . uh, because so many hunters trap the fox for their fur and others in our town see them as really bad and that we should kill them because they can destroy property. I mean, I guess they do destroy gardens and chicken coops and things, and they do chase the pheasants. Uh, but maybe if we learned about them, people could change their mind about the red fox. And, uh, they have dens and little fox babies called pups, and—"

"Thank you, Elita. We need to move on. Now, for the rest of you, we've been talking about your science projects due in November, and I want to share with you today some examples of a great project idea from the past. Now Elita is far ahead of us because she knows her topic and might already have her hypothesis. She's beginning data collection. Now some of you are worried about this project . . ."

I heard people whispering. *Not fair. She's so weird. I hate science projects. Foxes have rabies. Elita probably has rabies. You can't test if a fox can tell time. That's a stupid project. I'm going to build a volcano—*

I whipped my head around in anger. I saw Lindsay glaring at me with narrowed eyes and a clenched jaw. She looked like she actually wanted to hurt me. I snapped my head back to the front of the class where Mr. Dale pulled up a slide presentation about students in the past studying growth rates of bean plants and under what conditions mold will grow on certain foods.

"Can it be a group project?" someone asked behind me.

"You may have partners or a group of three," Mr. Dale said, "but you have to prove an equal division of labor with clearly assigned tasks for each group member. Data collection, the research report, and the representation of the data." He held up three fingers and then repositioned his glasses.

Out of the corner of my eye, I saw several hands shoot up in the air.

"Yes, Stephen?" Mr. Dale said and pointed to where he sat three rows behind me.

"Can I be in Elita's group? I want to study the red fox." I sucked in my breath. *Did that really just happen? Me?*

"Me too," called Allie from the right side of the room where she sat in the front row. "I choose Elita's group. That's final—Stephen, me, and Elita."

"Well," said Mr. Dale, "you'll have to present your argument to Elita about why she should bring you on as her scientific assistants. She'd be the lead scientist, but you'd both have to work to earn your grade. In fact, let's break up into pairs or groups of three and start brainstorming your observed phenomena. I'll bring us back together in ten minutes. Move your desks if you have to."

Stephen and Allie dragged their seats over to me. They both talked at once about how they'd promise to join me in data collection and how Stephen would research all about foxes and hunters. Allie reminded me that she would bring pork buns and her mother's sweet rice balls—all I wanted. I kept repeating Mr. Dale's words in my head that I was the "lead scientist." He always used super adult words when he talked to us. I loved that. I didn't feel like a baby in his class.

"When does he come? When can we see him?" Allie asked.

"Every night at 6:07. But I have a job and it might be hard to meet up on school nights. But on the weekends, we could." I liked bragging about my job. I felt grown up.

"Okay, let's start Saturday night. I'll bring dinner for everyone," Allie offered. "Would your mom be okay with that? How many people are in your family?"

"Four," I said slowly. Everything was happening so quickly.

"Where do you live, exactly?" Stephen asked.

"Up on Siler's Ridge—on Siler's Road. The brown house that's like a cabin. Black chimney. A porch with a swing."

"Good. I know where that is. I can ride my bike there."

"Okay," I said. "Maybe come at 5:30. And Mr. Dale said I'm supposed to think about why the fox might start changing his schedule mid-September. Why would he do that?"

"I have no idea," Stephen said. "Does he get cold or something? It gets cold at night soon."

"I'll research," Allie said. "And I promise I will work so hard and do everything you tell me to do. Please let us join your group, please!"

"Why do you guys care so much about my fox project?" I suddenly felt embarrassed. I wanted to make excuses about my house, my life in the woods. *My house is small. Not like Margo's. We have enough, but you'll think I'm poor. You'll think it's simple and boring.*

"I love foxes. In Chinese culture they can be good or bad based on how you view them. And they're always magical in Chinese fairy tales. I'll bring my books. I'll tell you more later. Hey, that would be cool—like a report on what foxes symbolize in every culture?"

"Maybe," I said. It didn't sound very scientific. "Most people think foxes are bad—like evil or something."

"I just like hanging out in the woods," Stephen said. "And foxes are cool. They're smart, right? You know that saying about being clever as a fox?"

The bell rang. "See you on Saturday night! I can stay till 9:00 if we want to hang out. That's my curfew because I have church on Sunday morning," Allie said.

"I'll see if my dad can pick me up 'cause I'll have my bike," Stephen said.

"Don't worry about it. My dad can get you home," Allie said. "See you Saturday."

"Bye," I said slowly. I didn't move. Maybe I was in shock. "Bye," I said again to Stephen as he looked at me and nodded with one hand raised to say goodbye. "We can roast marshmallows," I said, brightening up inside. "I have a fire pit."

73

"That's the best," Stephen said.

It would almost be like a party. And a cute boy would be there. I watched Stephen rush out of class.

I looked at my watch. 1:40. I had a cozy feeling inside.

That night at dinner, I finally talked to my parents about school. My dad told Cally that I "had the floor" and she couldn't interrupt even once. I told them about science class and how Stephen and Allie begged to be in my group. I told them how Mrs. Wu would bring us all dinner Saturday night by 5:30.

"I know," Mom said. "Mrs. Wu called this afternoon. I think she didn't realize the game land boundaries are up the ravine after you cross Spring Creek. I think she pictured hunters on our property. She asked all about this fox and whether Allie would be safe. I think she imagined your fox jumping up and biting you all out there in the yard and giving you rabies."

"She has a point," Dad said slowly. "I don't want you getting too close to the fox."

CHAPTER 11

DATA

Sometimes, my parents are just the best ever. My mom arranged for Cally to spend the evening and stay overnight at her friend's house, so she wouldn't bother me and my friends when 5:30 came around. And not only that, but my dad set up a table by the firepit with chocolate bars, graham crackers, and marshmallows for later in the evening. He'd already hauled over logs and kindling to build a great fire. On the back porch, my mom set our outside table with a pitcher of lemonade and napkins and forks. "I figured your dad and I could have a quiet dinner inside alone," she explained, "while you kids get to work outside. We won't bother you."

I wiped my sweating hands on my jeans and started pacing around the backyard.

"Elita, come here," my mom said. "Can I please braid your hair?" She stood on the porch with a brush and hair ties. I sat down and pulled my knees to my chest as my mom leaned down and braided my hair. My dad stood silently with his arms crossed as he looked into the woods.

"Dad? What should I do if the fox doesn't come? I mean the whole project is this fox. And we've been out here all afternoon, and maybe he smells us and won't come hunting. And maybe this will just waste Stephen and Allie's time. Oh! This is not a good idea!" I wrangled free of Mom's work on my hair, stood up, and started pacing again and wiping my hands on my jeans.

"That will be *data*," my dad said. "That reminds me: the scale is three feet to one inch. We can change that if you want to build a replica of the backyard or something. Do you want me to get graph paper for everyone?"

"Good idea."

♥ ♥ ♥

Allie arrived at my dirt driveway and let her mom cover her with bug spray. She waved her hands in front of her face and coughed. She lugged two bags full of Chinese food to the door.

Allie was a *talker*. I sat at the table and poured lemonade as she *talked and talked* about her little brother and her morning spent at the catering business with her mom. You know how I believe people have signature sandwiches; well, people also have signature expressions, and Allie liked to talk about the future and say, "I probably will one day." Like she talked about all her classes and how Mrs. Crisp inspired her to write stories and how she *probably would one day*. She said she loved my house and how the woods were all around. But she said she wanted a big apartment in New York City and she *probably would one day*. And Allie was really into having good manners. She put her napkin in her lap because it was good manners. She waited to serve up our pork buns and noodles because it was good manners to wait for Stephen. And then she said she'd now ask me a few questions because it was good manners to ask other people questions, too, and not do all the talking yourself.

"Don't you think Stephen is so cute?" she asked. "I mean, he's not my crush. I've been in love with Cole Enlow since first grade. He *will* notice me this year."

I could feel my face heat up. I knew it was becoming the color of my burnt orange sweater with my neon orange vest over it. I didn't have to answer though, because the back door opened, and my mom announced that Stephen was here.

Sweaty and beaming, Stephen said, "Good, I'm starving," as he practically threw himself into a chair. He wore his Penn State baseball cap and a blue hoodie. "Oh, wait!" he said and stuck a finger up in the air. "I gotta wash my hands."

I smiled. I loved how he used his hands to talk. I loved how he told my mom, "Thank you for having us over, Mrs. Brown."

Allie leaned over and said, "Good manners," and winked at me.

⬦ ⬦ ⬦

I told them everything I knew so far about my fox. When I talked about the fox, it's like everything else faded into the background. I wasn't nervous. I wasn't insecure. It's like I became a different person. I told Stephen and Allie that I wished to learn more about him and to figure out what our county thought about the foxes. I knew that hunters trap them.

"Can I be the person who writes the report about the red fox?" Allie asked. "I can even make a vocabulary page because last night I learned the words *vermin, ecosystem,* and *crepuscular.*"

"Huh?" Stephen and I said together. We looked at each other and laughed.

Allie stood up like she was giving us a lecture. "*Vermin* is the noun people use to describe the fox. It's the word you use for wild creatures people considered harmful because they carry diseases or destroy livestock and crops. You know, like rats or cockroaches or something. The word *vermin* usually makes people think about an offensive or annoying creature. Foxes are considered trouble. Like they don't belong, like there's no place for them at all."

"No!" Stephen said. "That's like discrimination."

Vermin. I hated the word. It even sounded evil.

"And *crepuscular* means active at dusk or twilight—you know, around sunset. So the fox is a *crepuscular* creature. Oh, and an *ecosystem* is like the whole network of living things and how they connect out there in the woods."

"I definitely think you should write our report," I said. "But make sure you include fun stuff like how a fox has a contact signal—a real hello—when he meets a friend. Guess what he says? He says, *Wow! Wow! Wow!* like a hoot owl!" I added, "And guess what else? The red fox hunts by jumping high into the air and steering himself with his tail. He jumps like sixteen feet or something. That's crazy. Oh, and I have some words for your vocabulary list."

"Cool," Stephen said. Then he furrowed his brow and rested his chin on his fist. "But if Allie writes our report, and you're doing the hypothesis and data, what do I do? I mean besides making sure you both have fun."

"My dad thinks we should make a diorama—like reproduce my backyard on a big board that we decorate with trees and grass and then mark the trail of the fox. And if he changes his pattern at all, we could mark it with red string where he goes. You could help build the diorama."

"That's awesome. I like that. Can I also ride my bike up here to help with data collection on the weekends? I'm like ten minutes away. I could just zoom up before dinner and zoom back home."

My face felt hot again. I pretended to stare out into the woods. "That would be fine," I said, while inside I was jumping around, squealing, and doing the Margo clap of joy.

"Okay," Allie said. "And another thing I'm thinking about— like another question for our project—is if animals have special patterns and routines, what happens if Siler's Ridge gets developed for shopping malls or houses? What happens to the red fox if something disrupts his pattern?"

"That's good," I said. "But these woods border the game lands. I think they are protected, but I'm not sure."

"What are those?" Allie asked.

"You know. The *game lands*. All this forest out there—and the meadow, creek, and woods on the other side, maybe ten thousand acres of it—are managed by the Pennsylvania Game Commission. Nobody can develop it because it's for hunting and fishing. And trapping. So the fox is a target out here." I was surprised that Allie didn't already know all this. She lived in town, right next to the university, but just like Margo, lived in a separate world from the houses away from town and nearer to the woods.

"Oh," Allie said. "Are there hunters out there now? Are we going to get shot?"

"The actual hunting area is marked down there way past the creek. The game land boundary doesn't start for a while. But yes, it's small game season right now. And bear season—with bows and muzzleloaders. Why do you think my dad makes me wear this neon orange fleece?"

"I thought you were a Clemson fan," Stephen said.

"Bears?" Allie said with widened eyes. "Okay, I've heard enough. You both collect the data. I'll be home in my safe house in the heart of town away from danger."

I looked at my watch. 6:00 p.m.

"Okay, guys. Let's sit on the porch quietly. The fox comes at 6:07 on the dot."

I pulled out my field journal and pen from my back pocket and waited.

"I'm so nervous," Allie whispered.

"This is so awesome," Stephen added.

"Can I record this on my phone?" Allie whispered. She held her phone up and pressed record. "Where should I point my phone?"

"Over by that oak tree at the very edge of our property. He'll cross there, move along the tree line, and go into the understory to pick up the trail to the meadow."

"What's an understory?" Allie asked quietly. "I'll add that to my vocabulary list."

"The plants on the forest floor."

We all held our breath.

I don't know why, but at that moment I thought about God. I prayed with all my heart that fox would appear—it was now 6:03.

Nobody spoke. Nobody moved. *Please God. Please God.*

Suddenly, the fox popped out from the understory and trotted along his path.

I looked down into my field journal. The fox had come *every night* at 6:07, and now 6:03?

"That's him! That's him!" Allie hissed.

Leading with his shiny black nose, dark red snout, and raised ears, the fox trotted happily in front of us. He acknowledged us briefly, just long enough for Allie to start recording on her phone. The black on his paws and legs looked like he wore little dark socks. I felt oddly proud of him with his bright white chest and enormous red and brown tail, tipped with white like he dipped it in a can of paint. We watched him slip into the understory of red sumac and fern. I imagined the way his paws felt on the soft green moss as he padded away from us.

Stephen broke the silence. We were quiet and filled with awe.

"That's awesome! That's crazy! What's he doing? Where is he going? How did he choose that trail? Why was he early? Oh my gosh, I *love that fox*," he burst out with his hands on his head. "Allie, would you please email me the video so I can show my little brothers?"

I laughed and hopped up and down a few times, just like I would on Christmas morning.

"Come on, you guys! I can show you some more cool stuff."

I led them down the trail past the Burgley house and then on to Spring Creek. At first, Allie complained as Stephen and I dragged her into the woods, but soon her eyes were sparkling as we walked along mossy trails with ferns rustling in the cool evening air. The setting sun lit us all up like angels, and we balanced on fallen logs over the chiming creek. We sat on a log over the creek and let our feet dangle down. Just like I knew they would, three deer approached Spring Creek to drink—most likely a mother and her almost grown fawns. Allie started to record video again.

"I cannot believe people shoot them," Stephen whispered.

"I know," Allie said.

"Well, the meat of one deer is like fifty pounds of venison. It will feed a family all winter. And it's good," I said. "Well, at least the venison sausage is good. And the chili. My dad is friends with hunters, and sometimes we buy the meat."

"But doesn't it make you sad? Like would you ever eat fox meat?" Allie asked.

"Yeah. I guess it does." I paused. "It really does make me sad."

We balanced on the log back to land and started to walk back to my backyard. We passed the part of the woods I called my fort where I'd dragged branches and old logs to make a little house. It's where I'd bring my stuffed animals and play make-believe. Ugh. I heard Lindsay's voice at Margo's party: *She's a baby.*

Stephen noticed the fort and raced through branches and ferns to get to it. "Is this yours, EB?" he hollered back to Allie and me.

I smiled. A nickname. "Yeah," I stammered. "From when I was a kid. I'm not done yet."

"Want any help finishing it?"

Allie elbowed me and giggled. "Like a date in the woods," she whispered. "Say yes, fast."

"Yes!" I hollered back. "Yes!"

When we returned to my yard, a warm fire awaited us in our fire pit. We made s'mores and laughed as Stephen burned anything he could—including the marshmallows that he loved to watch melt in the fire. And we talked. We all had either a little brother or little sister to complain about. We all had parents who made us do too many chores. We all had corny jokes to share. We joked about Mrs. Crisp and how Mr. Dale got way too excited about raccoon droppings. We laughed so hard I almost choked on my s'more.

But we didn't talk about *everything*.

I mean, the one thing I wished I could talk about, but didn't know how to, was those high-top tables in the lunchroom. Where did Stephen go during every lunch period? And why did Allie seem so carefree at school, flitting around any table she wanted? Girls like her fit in everywhere, but I still didn't fit anywhere. The only place I really belonged was in the woods with my fox.

"You know what I was thinking?" Stephen said as he zipped up his hoodie when Allie said her dad had arrived to drive them home. "I was thinking that if the fox goes down that trail every evening, he must come *back*, right? I mean he has to get back to where he started in order to go down the trail again, right?"

"Right."

"So when does that happen? When does he come back? A fox can't predict ahead of time what kind of rodents or birds he'll get or when, right? But wouldn't it be cool to see if he returned at the same time at night, too?"

"I'll stay up and watch tonight."

"Thanks, EB!" Stephen said. He fist-bumped my hand.

CHAPTER 12

HYPOTHESIS

Mr. Dale was right. Something strange was happening with my fox. I'd collected ten more days of data, and the fox was crossing earlier and earlier.

"What's he doing?" I demanded as I burst through the door of his classroom. I practically slammed my Field Notes journal down on his desk and then put my hands on my head. "I mean—is this random? Sometimes 6:07, sometimes 6:00, sometimes 5:55."

I showed him my chart with the date, the time, and even the weather. I had been taking such good notes.

"What do you notice about the times?"

"Decreasing."

"Right. Well, there's something you haven't added to your chart. You've looked at day, time, weather, but is there anything else you notice changing outside? Something that might relate to time or even temperature."

Just then, Allie and Stephen scrambled into the classroom as Allie called out, "I think I know the answer! I think I know what's happening!" She held her hand up in the air like she wanted Mr. Dale to call on her.

"Hold on a minute—let me get Mrs. Harlow in here," Mr. Dale said.

I froze. The eighth grade science teacher sort of scared me. Mrs. Jasmine Harlow was a total *boss*. Whenever I saw her in the hallway, I thought she looked like a movie star. Today she wore high heels and a leopard print dress. As she entered the classroom, we respectfully made way for her.

"Tell me about this fox," she said.

I couldn't find my words as I looked up at Mrs. Harlow towering over our notebooks. Finally, Allie spoke.

"Well, he has this evening ritual—the same trail he walks on every single night at the same time, for a while, but then he's crossing Elita's backyard in these random ways, but like a little earlier every single night. And I think I know why."

"I think I also know why," Mrs. Harlow said, "and it will be fantastic to prove it."

"What is it?" Stephen and I asked at the same time. He punched me gently in the arm and said, "Jinx."

"Sunset," Allie said. Her voice sounded reverent and quiet.

I nodded. *The sun did set earlier in autumn. The nights seemed longer and colder, too. But why? Come to think of it, why do we have seasons at all?*

"Ladies and gentlemen, please follow me into my laboratory," Mrs. Harlow said. We obediently trotted after her. What followed was the most mind-blowing explanation of how the earth orbits around the sun on this tilted axis. As it travels and tilts away from the sun, we have autumn and then winter. Less sunlight. More darkness.

"Here we are now in mid-September. What do you notice?"

"It's darker sooner as it rotates. The sun will set sooner and sooner," Allie answered.

"And our fox travels sooner and sooner. He's telling time by the sun," I said. "Oh my goodness, that's so cool."

"So the fox decides to start hunting based on the time the sun sets? That's how he tells time?" Stephen asked. "But how do we mark the time the sun sets exactly? If we could know that, we could see if the time the fox crosses Elita's backyard—how many minutes before the sun goes down—matches the sunset time. We'd just subtract to see, right—to see if it's the same amount of minutes before the sun every night. So cool."

"Astronomers. Meteorologists. Here, look." Mrs. Harlow pressed print on her laptop, reached over to her printer, and then handed me a chart of sunset times from September 1 till last night.

"Awesome. This is so awesome," I said.

"Get to work," Mrs. Harlow said. "And be sure to tell me your results. I'm invested in this fox now."

We walked back to Mr. Dale's classroom and settled into our seats. I couldn't wait to start comparing my fox's schedule to the sunset. Nothing else mattered—not the lunchroom, not how out of place I felt. I was focused and curious. I took a deep breath and smiled.

But then Allie tapped me on the shoulder and leaned over to

whisper in my ear. "Don't go into the girls' bathroom."

"Why not?" I whispered back.

"Just trust me." Her face looked sad but also angry and determined. "I'll tell you later."

CHAPTER 13

MRS. BURGLEY'S SECRET

October in Pennsylvania looks like a forest full of fireworks frozen overhead. You walk underneath gold, burgundy, red, orange, bright yellow, and even purple explosions. And with a bright blue sky overhead, you feel like you're swallowed up in color.

The air turned so crisp that I raked the Burgleys' leaves in my fleece jacket and mittens. Mrs. Burgley would come over to me with a mug of hot apple cider and ginger snaps and tell me what a hard worker I was. But it didn't feel like it was work out there as I sipped cider and tried not to spill it when Bo and Bee ran circles around me. And I even felt guilty when Mr. Burgley handed me my one hundred dollars every Saturday in September. I would've worked for the Burgleys for free.

On the first Saturday of October, Mrs. Burgley said we'd also start the inside work of sorting her things for donations or the trash.

I imagined the Burgley home would smell musty and old and full of hoarded papers and trinkets. I had never been inside yet; our Saturday lunch always involved eating ham sandwiches on the porch with Oreo cookies and potato chips, which I gobbled up after working for three hours spreading fresh mulch in their front beds and helping Mrs. Burgley arrange pots of orange mums on her front porch and sidewalk. We were supposed to make the front yard look ready for potential buyers.

But when I stepped inside, I smiled as I inhaled the warm smell of baking apples and fresh bread. Mrs. Burgley stood in a pure white kitchen with shiny silver pots hanging overhead. Everything was bright and tidy and organized. I loved her style—like the blue bowl of shiny red apples on the counter and the bouquet of dried blue hydrangeas in the middle of the big oak table. She stirred apple cider on the stove and told me a pie was in the oven for after lunch.

In their living room, Mr. Burgley sat reading a book next to their wood-burning stove in a large brown recliner. The Penn State pregame show was on in the background. This room, too, was clean and sparse with just a cream-colored couch that held big pillows and several crocheted blankets and a wooden coffee table. I couldn't imagine what I'd need to sort and organize in a house this clean.

I always thought my house was clean, but this? I recalled Cally's pile of dance shoes and my own stack of books and homework on the kitchen table. I thought of my mom's craft projects in the living room. A basket of unfolded laundry was usually sitting at the bottom of the stairs, and we scattered our library books we were done with on the stairs themselves—reminders to take them back by their due dates. I wanted a place like the Burgleys' house one day—open and clean and cozy and simple. I wanted Mr. Burgley's big window that overlooked Spring Creek. Their house made me want to ask my mom if I could redecorate my room in cream colors with crisp white curtains.

Mrs. Burgley led me into a room in the back of the house—their library. Now I understood my task as I looked at floor-to-ceiling bookshelves and what looked like *thousands* of books.

Mrs. Burgley sat down carefully into a light brown armchair in the corner of the room. She placed her mug of cider on a small table beside the chair.

"Now. Here's the task: I need help sorting. I'm hoping you'll bring me stacks of books and I'll tell you which ones are keepers. If it's not a keeper, you'll put it in one of these boxes. When it's full, you'll bring it to Mr. Burgley's truck."

"Seems easy enough," I said.

"This work is a little past us," she said. "If I get on the floor, I can't get back up again. If I fall off the ladder to reach the top shelves, the fall could end me. My back isn't strong enough to carry the boxes, and Irvin shouldn't do it either. And I'm not even hearing as well as I used to." She paused, then added, "It's hard to feel young on the inside and old on the outside. As a matter of fact, I think it's hard to feel anything on the inside that doesn't match what's happening on the outside. Does that make any sense to you at all? Sometimes I don't always make sense."

I tilted my head up and chewed my lip, thinking about times the inside feelings don't match the outside things happening.

"I think so." And before I knew what was happening, I was kneeling down by Mrs. Burgley's chair and leaning in to make sure she could hear me. "I mean, I felt like I'd be popular in seventh grade and instead, I'm the opposite. People tease me about my fox project. Someone called me a baby. But inside, I felt like I was okay before school started. So I think I know what you mean."

She nodded and sipped her cider slowly.

"Seventh grade?"

"Yes."

"Hmm. That's right. I remember seventh grade."

I love it when adults don't ask too many questions. And Mrs. Burgley didn't ask me *one thing* about seventh grade. Instead, she said, "Bring me those dark blue books on the bottom shelf there—the whole stack."

"These?"

"Yes. Now let me see. Yes, this one. Take a look at that one."

She handed me a book, and on the front it read *Forest Ridge Middle School*. It was her yearbook from over sixty years ago. "Turn to the Gs. Look for Shirley Galvinson. You'll see me in seventh grade. Look at my hair! Look at my teeth jutting out."

"You're cute," I assured her, looking up from the yearbook picture to see Mrs. Burgley's current hair that now seemed more like white spun cotton candy than the dark curled hair held back with a headband in the photo. Back then, she wore a cardigan sweater and a crisp white blouse.

"That was one of the worst years of my life," she said and closed her eyes. She leaned back against the chair and put her hand over her chest like she was in actual pain. She took a deep breath. "Oh, how I wish I knew the secret I know now back then."

"The secret?"

"Yes. It's something I learned years later that helped heal that ache I carried around all my life."

"Did someone die?" I blurted out. *What happened to Mrs. Burgley that would hurt her that much?*

"No—nothing like that. It's a small thing that became a big thing."

I waited. I didn't speak. I flipped the pages of her yearbook to see all the black-and-white photos of cheerleaders and athletes, and other activities like Math Team, Glee Club, and the school newspaper. It seemed a lot like my school if you ignored the fashion and hair styles in the pictures.

"Well," she said slowly.

She looked at me. Her eyes—her whole face—reminded me of my fox. I can't explain it. I imagined those sparkles again swirling up in the air around us. I guess when I start imagining sparkles, it means something really wonderful is happening.

"It's just that lunchroom." She paused. Her face gleamed. I shivered even though it wasn't cold.

The lunchroom?

"I didn't have a seat in there. My best friends grew up faster than I did, and they just left me behind. They moved into popularity, and I stayed back alone. I read my book alone at a table. I was an avid reader." Mrs. Burgley looked at me. She squinted her eyes, assessing me.

I snapped my head up. *The seat. How was it possible that Mrs.*

Burgley understood about the tables? Should I tell her? Should I tell her how Allie called to tell me someone wrote "Elita has rabies" in the girls' bathroom? How I'd been crying at night about my seat at those high-top tables? I thought the fox would make me special, but he only gave me an enemy I couldn't identify. Lindsay? Margo? Some jealous eighth grader from Mrs. Harlow's class?

"But I learned something a few years ago—" She stopped.

"Yes?" I prompted.

"It's the secret. But it's hard to explain. It's something mature, something deeply true but hard to understand." Mrs. Burgley now looked at me as if she were evaluating whether I could handle a difficult concept. She raised her head up and squinted her eyes again, judging me. Now, she looked *exactly* the way my fox looked at me that first day.

I sat up as tall as I could. I said, "I'm one of the smartest girls in my grade—even in math, which I don't really like."

"I see."

"And I'm a good listener." I tried to think of other things to qualify me to learn the secret. "And I can keep a secret," I finally said.

"This isn't a secret to *keep*. It's a secret you must *tell* once you learn it."

I waited in silence until she said, "I like that you're confident. I like that you're starting to know yourself. I like that in a girl. What I mean about the secret is how abstract it is. It's something *spiritual*. Let me think on it. Let me pray on it. Monday afternoon, I'll tell you."

"I have to wait till *Monday*?"

"Waiting is good. Patience is good. It builds character." Mrs.

Burgley stood up. "Now let's get to work. I want all those year-books in the keeper boxes. But the travel guides on the shelf above you can toss in the donation boxes."

I carried boxes out to their truck while Mr. Burgley cheered me on from his seat in the living room. Finally, right around noon, he called us to the big kitchen table where he set out grilled cheese and tomato slices. When I told them I like to put the tomatoes *in* my grilled cheese, along with some dill, Mr. Burgley said, "Now that's a sandwich!"

CHAPTER 14

A BULLY

I know this is weird, but I like having school on a rainy, dark day. It gives me a cozy feeling inside to see the windows weep with water droplets and to hear the patter of rain on the roof. I love it when all the students sit at their desks and work quietly. I don't know—I just feel safe. Everything feels right and organized.

That's how it felt on Monday. Until I remembered those lunch tables. It's like there were two of me: the fox girl and the girl who wanted a seat at the popular table. I wanted both. And sometimes I just couldn't control my bad moods. I think that's the problem with not getting a seat at the table you want; it makes everything else in life feel wrong. Even when you do have good things happening, you just can't see them.

Some thoughts I can't keep out of my mind. They play on a loop like something's stuck in my brain. I couldn't stop replaying that day Margo told me *this seat's saved*. I'd see Margo and her new group of friends—including Lindsay—laughing in the hallway in front of their lockers, and I'd walk by, invisible. I'd see Kee holding her field hockey bag while the soccer boys joked around and asked about her weekend. I'd walk by, invisible. The worst part is that everyone else seemed to have so much fun. They seemed happy. That's what popularity meant to me. I wanted happiness and laughter and that feeling that everyone wants to circle around you and hear what you have to say. Popularity means love, attention, and *being somebody*.

I was nobody.

And with all my after-school work with the Burgleys and my fox project, I had no time to reinvent myself. My dad put all the money he could in my college savings account. He was determined that I was going to college even though he never got to. But what's the point of new clothes and makeup if nobody you care about is ever going to see them? *I'm invisible.*

I know what you're thinking. What about that great time with Allie and Stephen? What about all the attention from the teachers? Well, it was good but also bad. The whole fox project made Lindsay Myers really mad for some reason. She not only spread the rumor that I was a baby and most likely wrote bad things about me on the bathroom mirror, but she snarled at me every time I said anything in Nature Club or science class. When Mr. Dale praised me for my hypothesis that the fox's timing on his hunting trail would stay the same even through changing weather, Lindsay whispered behind me, "She is the *worst*. We get it. You're so smart, Elita."

I confirmed the truth in Monday's Nature Club: I had a bully after me.

Mr. Dale said he'd test us on leaf identification based on the shape, size, and color of the leaves he held up before he let us loose to find them ourselves in the woods. I knew them all—the red maple, the white oak, and the ginkgo. When everyone else guessed pine, I knew it was eastern hemlock.

"How do you know all these, Elita?" Mr. Dale said after I knew the difference between a Norway maple and sugar maple.

"Well, I help my mom with her leaf cut-outs for bulletin boards, for one. She's a teacher, too. And I also just like them, I guess. I like to do crayon rubbings over them. I mean, I like to know the names of things. And the sugar maple is burnt orange in fall, so that's easy to spot. The Norway maple has that golden yellow with just some bright orange at the tips," I explained. "So right there," I said and pointed down the trail. "See?"

"See?" Lindsay mocked in a baby voice. A few of the boys beside her laughed. I thought of how much she had tried to get Mr. Dale's attention with all her stories of hiking in the Rocky Mountains, but here in Pennsylvania, he wanted to talk about native, local things.

"What's this one, Elita?" Stephen said, holding up a deep purple leaf.

"White ash."

"This?" Mr. Dale said and held up a pumpkin-orange leaf.

"Buckeye."

Lindsay folded her arms and glared at me.

"What I appreciate," Mr. Dale said, "is how each leaf has a different shape and different expression in autumn, and together, they make this beautiful forest." He waved his hand to direct our attention to the trees.

"Just like us?" Stephen said with wide, mocking eyes. "Are you going to start telling us how we all look different but how we are all beautiful in our own way?" He pretended to gag, and I added, "Ugh."

"If you two don't start walking down that trail and finding some leaves, I just might," Mr. Dale said and swatted Stephen on his hat with his buckeye leaf.

Later, in science class, Allie and Stephen told everyone about my fox and how he traveled *exactly* one hour before sunset. I listened and smiled at them. I wished I could talk to people as easily as Allie and as confidently as Stephen. But it was okay. We were a group, and they loved the fox like I did. I heard people ask Allie to make more videos for her TikTok.

I couldn't wait to get back into the woods on my way to the Burgley house after school. I closed my notebook as the bell rang, just as I heard a low voice saying my name. I whipped around to see Lindsay leaning over to two girls.

"Elita had rabies," she said, and the two girls beside her laughed. "Rabies makes you crazy. It makes you hallucinate."

CHAPTER 15

A SEAT AT THE TABLE

I lugged piles of *National Geographic* magazines into boxes in the Burgleys' library. I thought about Lindsay. *Why does she hate me? Why is she so mean? I mean—she's really pretty and she's already popular. She's friends with Margo and Kee. She wears these cool hiking boots. I wish I had hiking boots like that. I wish I had hair like hers.*

I'd only been working for twenty minutes when Mrs. Burgley entered the library with a silver tray of hot apple cider and a plate of ginger snaps.

"Let's take a break."

"Okay," I said and joined her by the large window that over-looked the forest. In the distance, I could see a buck walking down to Spring Creek. I didn't tell Mrs. Burgley. I kept it all to myself. My mom says that my greatest flaw is *keeping things to yourself.* Mom wishes I would talk to her more, but I just can't. I don't know why. Maybe it *is* my greatest flaw. My mom believes everyone has a fatal flaw. In English class, Mrs. Crisp said that heroes often have fatal flaws that end up causing their downfall. Flaws like pride, too much curiosity, or falling in love with the wrong person.

"I thought about how to tell you the secret." She held her steaming mug of cider in both hands, like a child. "The lunchroom situation. Where were we?"

"The part about not having a seat. Your friends were popular and you read alone at your lunch table." *See, I was a good listener.*

"Yes. It's a scar. It stays with you. I wish I could tell you how what is happening to you doesn't stay with you. But it does. Every table you don't get to sit at will remind you." She closed her eyes and sipped her cider. Then she looked out the window, distracted by something in the distance.

"Elita! Look! Oh, just look at him. So magnificent! The king of the forest. Such joy to see a buck with those antlers. He's just magnificent."

The same buck I saw now wandered near the Burgley house. I like how older people say things like *magnificent.*

"Where was I?" she said after a few minutes of watching the buck.

"The tables—the tables you can't sit at."

"The tables. Yes. It starts in the lunchroom. You don't have a seat with the popular girls. Then you don't have a seat at whatever table you think will make you happy—like with the athletes or the singers or the rich or famous people. And you keep thinking that if only you had a seat there, you'd be truly, truly happy. You'd be okay inside."

I nodded. I *had* been thinking that. So far, I understood everything she said.

"And the seat you want changes. You'll wonder why everyone else is seated with a boyfriend and later a husband. You'll wonder why people have better houses or better careers or better children. It's a terrible, terrible way to live." She looked at me a moment to see if I was following. I nodded. She went on.

"It's terrible because you feel wrong and bad inside even though you haven't done anything. You can't make it right. You just feel like everyone is judging you and you are not ever going to be okay. I wasted a lot of my life fighting for a seat at the table—until maybe when I was an adult. That's why I don't know if you'll understand me. But I *want* you to understand."

"I'll try," I said.

Mrs. Burgley's face pleaded; she grasped her mug harder, and she pursed her lips. "It has to do with God. Are you okay if I talk about that?"

"Yes," I said. But I wasn't sure. We went to church on Sundays, but the whole time, I just thought about the crockpot mac-n-cheese waiting at home for lunch. I knew the stories of the Bible just like any kid in church—Adam and Eve, Noah's ark, Daniel in the lions' den—and we said a blessing before dinner. But we didn't really talk about God a lot.

And I even knew the whole part about needing Jesus to come into my heart and forgive me for the wrong things I did. But that was about it. I guess I didn't really think about God, if you want to know the truth. Well, I sort of did. I prayed for the fox to come when Stephen and Allie came that one day. Sometimes in the woods, I'd think about things like heaven or angels or magical things I couldn't see like fairies and gnomes. I'd think about invisible things that might be all around me. Was that faith? To believe in invisible things?

"When I was your mom's age, I kept thinking about the tables. I remembered that feeling of not having a seat. So think about that feeling, if it's not too painful in your heart. I think the word for it is shame. Shame is the feeling you feel. It makes you want to hide. You like to know the names of things, right?"

"Right." But how did she know that? And how did she know that I knew all about wanting to hide? I thought of how I hid in Margo's bathroom. I thought of how I hid my face in my folded arms in science class.

"At the same time, I was reading my Bible more and praying to God. I knew God loved me and wanted good things for my life, but I really didn't think about Jesus much of the time."

I nodded. I sipped the tart cider.

"And then I read something that was like a lightning bolt in my soul. I was sitting right where we are now when God spoke to me."

I had goosebumps all over my arms. The room felt cold. I both wanted to run away and stay right where I was forever. God spoke? Right here? I took a deep breath and looked out the window. I tried to imagine the voice of God and couldn't. *Does God speak to people?*

Mrs. Burgley reached for a tattered green book that, if handled roughly, would surely disintegrate. "Here's what I read." She turned to a spot near the end of the book. "Wait a second. Irvin! Irvin! Can you bring me my reading glasses?"

As we waited for Mr. Burgley, she told me that the Bible isn't like a typical book. She explained that you don't have to read it from start to finish. You can dip in and read where you want to, and God will speak to you through the words. But it's in your heart. The Holy Spirit. *Goosebumps again.*

The first part is history, then there's some poetry, some predictions about Jesus coming, and then all sorts of stories about Jesus, she was saying. Then you get letters some guy named Paul wrote. I was listening, but I was also worried why Mr. Burgley was taking so long. Finally, he poked his head into the library and delivered the glasses. Bo and Bee lazily followed him and then curled up on the floor beside Mrs. Burgley. The room cheered up. Every room cheers up when a dog comes in. Bo inched over to me and put his head in my lap.

There I was with a dog in my lap, bookshelves rising up like a protective fort around me, and Mrs. Burgley bothering to talk to someone as unimportant and invisible as I felt about *big ideas.* Like my soul. Like God. I didn't want to be anywhere else in the world. I scratched Bo's ears and watched his grateful eyes gazing up at me.

"It's in a letter Paul—who knew and loved Jesus—wrote to a church, and to us, about what we truly need to know most of all about *who we are.*"

I leaned in to listen. What would Paul say? Would God speak to me through the words like to Mrs. Burgley? Who was I? Even Bo perked up his ears to listen.

CHAPTER 16

SPARKLES IN MY SOUL

Mrs. Burgley turned to a letter called Ephesians. I thought Ephesians would make a good name for a dog. "I'll just read it. It's confusing maybe. But I have to read all of it to get to the part where God spoke to me. I'll pause after each part to see if you understand." She started reading in a voice that made me think she would have made a great kindergarten teacher. I don't care what anyone says. No matter how old you are, you're never too old to enjoy someone reading a book to you.

She read slowly: *"Once you were dead because of your disobedience and your many sins. You used to live in sin, just like the rest of the world, obeying the devil—the commander of the powers in the unseen world. He is the spirit at work in the hearts of those who refuse to obey God. All of us used to live that way, following the passionate desires and inclinations of our sinful nature. By our very nature we were subject to God's anger, just like everyone else."*

She peered at me over her reading glasses. "Do you understand that part? We're spiritually dead inside without Jesus. And we're full of sin—we cannot do the right thing."

"I think so," I said. But I wasn't thinking of me. I thought of Lindsay. I shivered because what if it was the devil at work in *her* heart? Then I *did* think of me. Was the devil in *my* heart? Hadn't I been secretly wishing for terrible things to happen to Kee, Margo, and Lindsay? I didn't like this so far. This wasn't fun to think about. I couldn't help feeling bad about myself. Then my thoughts were even worse. I thought of how I ignored Cally most of the time and how she made me jealous. I thought about how I really didn't like to talk to my mom. It was like a parade of memories of how bad I was marched through my brain. Ugh. I'm not a good person.

"It gets better," Mrs. Burgley promised. "And we're not to the part where I heard from God." She read very slowly and emphasized each word. *"But God is so rich in mercy, and he loved us so much, that even though we were dead because of our sins, he gave us life when he raised Christ from the dead. (It is only by God's grace that you have been saved!) For he raised us from the dead along with Christ and seated us with him in the heavenly realms because we are united with Christ Jesus. . . . For we are God's masterpiece. He has created us anew in Christ Jesus, so we can do the good things he planned for us long ago."*

She closed the Bible and folded her hands on top of it. "Did any pictures come into your mind when I read that?"

"The masterpiece part. It's like a painting."

"Yes—you are a masterpiece! But what about that other image?"

"Um—God raising me up to be with Him?" I guessed.

She read Ephesians 2 again and told me to listen for the word "seated."

"God seated us with Christ in the heavenly realms. That's the secret! It's already true of me right now. I am seated with Jesus at the greatest table—the one my heart really longs for. He's saving a seat for you, too, Elita. He makes you a new person inside and has good things planned for you to do with your life. I was sitting right here when Jesus told me He saved a seat for me. 'This seat's saved for you,' He said."

He's saving a seat for me. Goosebumps. Sparkles, but in my soul.

Bee came over to me. I scratched her behind her ears, and she came close to lick my face. Her tail thumped on the ground. I was listening hard. I wanted to hear an actual voice from heaven. Nothing. I closed my eyes. I did like that part where Jesus was *saving a seat for me.* I thought of walking to Jesus toward those high-top tables and instead of Margo's voice, I heard Jesus say, "This seat's saved . . . for Elita." I felt my eyes filling up with tears. My nose started to run, so I buried my face into Bee's fur to hide from Mrs. Burgley. Bo stayed in my lap, pinning me in place so I couldn't move, even if I wanted to.

"You don't need to have shame, Elita. God doesn't want you to hide. God forgives us and makes us clean inside. And you are marvelous just as you are; you don't need to try and be like any other girls. Jesus wants to be with you."

With me? And marvelous just as I am? I thought of the list of all the ways I was supposed to improve.

Mrs. Burgley continued. She leaned forward and stared into

my eyes, into my soul. "It's hard to picture. But it's true. You're seated with Jesus when you ask Him to come into your life, forgive your sin, and make you a new person. Remember, He cleans up your heart. You get a seat at His table. He saved it for you. I wish I would have known that, Elita. I could have walked into that seventh grade lunchroom and seen all those popular girls, and I could have known in my heart that I already had a seat at the best table with Jesus." Her eyes glistened now. Her nose would soon run like mine. I looked up from Bee's fur. Mrs. Burgley's face seemed lit up to me—radiant and joyful. Like her soul was sparkling.

I tried to picture my seat with Jesus. "But I'm right *here*," I finally said. "How can I also be *there*?"

"It's a mystery. I don't know—Paul was most likely in a Roman prison when he wrote that. That was his *here*. But he experienced himself as *there* with Jesus in that special seat."

I didn't say anything. I couldn't. I was trying to picture my seat with Jesus. First, I thought of an old metal folding chair—the kind in every school lunchroom. *That's not it.* Then I imagined a royal throne—gold with a red velvet seat. But instead of me, I saw a red fox seated there. *That's not it either.* Finally, I put myself in the royal seat. But not like a princess in a gown; I was a girl in sturdy hiking boots, a dark green jacket, and a beautiful yellow bow tying back my long brown hair. I wore a golden pendant with a fox hanging on it. Strong. Beautiful. The perfect mix of princess *and* naturalist.

"Elita—take this advice and put it in the middle of your heart," Mrs. Burgley told me. I was listening. "For the rest of your life, no matter what classroom, no matter what happens at a friend's house, no matter where you work or where you go, remember you are already seated with Christ, and He has a special place saved for you. So you never have to worry if you have a seat."

I remembered how I felt the day Margo invited Kee to make the crêpes and how grown up they acted. I didn't have a seat with the mature girls. *I could have thought about my seat with Jesus.* I thought of Margo's party when she opened the stuffed poodle and how everyone else was so glamorous. I didn't have a seat with the beautiful girls. *I could have thought about my seat with Jesus.*

If I asked Jesus right now, could I take my seat with Him? Could I think about that seat instead of the lunchroom seat? And every time I heard Margo's words, could I picture Jesus saying He saved a seat just for me?

I liked mysteries. I liked unexplainable, supernatural things. Like my fox. Maybe I could practice thinking of myself as part of another *realm*—another kingdom altogether. I mean, sometimes the forest did feel magical like that, like it was more than it actually was. Like unseen things like angels were in there.

I remember how Allie had told me something in school that I hadn't stopped thinking about. She told me that in Chinese culture, the fox is a shapeshifter. She called it the *huli jing* and told me that in Chinese folklore the fox can turn into a wise, old woman. I looked at Mrs. Burgley and the thought flickered through my mind that maybe . . . Was I in a Chinese fairy tale? No, of course not. I was too old for silly things like this. Even Cally was. I knew these things weren't true, animals can't turn into people, but I *did* know that God was true, and maybe He sent me my fox and Mrs. Burgley.

111

I felt amazed. I felt suddenly part of something supernatural—but not a fairy tale. I was learning something true and more real than I could understand. I pictured my throne. Now I pictured the fox sitting by my feet, like a royal assistant.

"I like the part where you said Jesus saved a seat for me," I said. "I like it so much."

"You can start reading the Bible for yourself, you know. Jesus is a friend, and like any friend, you have to spend time and get to know Him. You have to have conversations, and the Bible is what helps you do this. And you'll like it."

I nodded.

"You know—there's a part in the Bible where God sends ravens to help a prophet. It's like how God sent you your fox. Do you have a Bible of your own?"

"Yes," I said. *Did God send me my fox? Did God send my mom into the grocery store at the exact time to meet Mrs. Burgley where she could ask about my coming to work for her?*

I did have a Bible, it's just that I never read it.

CHAPTER 17

GOING VIRAL

I made neat columns in my Field Notes journal that listed the *day, time, weather,* and *sunset.* I showed Mr. Dale and Mrs. Harlow my notes during lunch as I sat on my usual stool at the scientific drawing station. I explained to Mr. Dale that not only would we consider if a fox sticks to a tight schedule, but we would also see if his schedule was dependent on weather.

"Is it?" he asked and rubbed his chin. "Hold on a moment. I want to gather the other teachers in here." Two other teachers besides Mrs. Harlow crowded around my stool. They used words I didn't understand like *dependent variables* and *statistical analysis.* "That fox only varies his timing by less than twenty-two seconds if we average this. And other variables matter little. Fascinating."

"Can we see this fox?" Mrs. Harlow asked. I closed my journal and shook my head.

"I . . . I don't have any pictures. But Allie made videos and posted them on her channel." I felt like a baby again. Mrs. Harlow didn't seem like she was judging me, but she took out her phone, searched for Allie's name, found her channel, and pulled up the first video of us watching the fox cross my backyard.

"Whoa. Wait a minute," Mrs. Harlow said. "What is happening? Dale, the video had 56,000 views. Look!" The teachers gathered around to watch Allie narrate her one-minute video. Allie spoke like a reporter and said, "Reporting from Elita's backyard, we're here waiting for the approach of the fox."

"Looks like your fox is going viral," Mr. Dale said and smiled.

"Have you considered submitting your research? To the Wildlife Council or even *National Geographic*? Maybe to the Game Commission? What about—" Mrs. Harlow was full of suggestions.

"That's a great idea," Mr. Dale said. "I think Elita and her team care most about protecting the fox. This project could halt any development along Siler's Ridge—fracking, drilling, or even housing or retail up there. Would you, Allie, and Stephen make a video on this same page and tag the Game Commission?"

"Um, my mom doesn't let me go online on my phone," I stammered. "She says I'm too young and it's bad for my brain." I tried to explain, but I felt like a little kid again. I felt like I did when I showed up in jeans while everyone else at the party had on their dresses.

"Smart woman," Mrs. Harlow said. "It's all just videos and pictures making people jealous, unless, of course, you use your page for education. I deleted my Instagram because it just makes me feel bad." *Mrs. Harlow? Feel bad?*

"Allie can do it," I offered.

"Your mom knows that everyone's just bragging and trying to feel good about themselves on social media. It's a terrible source of self-esteem. You're on the right path, Elita Brown." Mrs. Harlow looked down at me as I thought about Margo and her posts about her outfits. Did Margo not feel good about herself otherwise? *Hypothesis: People use social media to brag because they don't feel good inside.*

I sat alone and drew a picture of the fox with Mr. Dale's special pencils. I had another hypothesis. I was a lead scientist, a naturalist, but I also believed that God sent my fox, even though it didn't sound very scientific. I think science and God can go together, can't they? So here it goes: *Hypothesis: My fox is related to God somehow. There's such a thing as the supernatural.*

❡ ❡ ❡

Every Saturday and Sunday in October, Stephen rode his bike to my house. On Saturdays he always wore the same blue hoodie and Penn State baseball cap. On Sundays he wore a Pittsburgh Steelers jersey. I always wore my orange fleece and jeans. "We are people of routine," Stephen said and laughed. "We are foxes."

My dad and Stephen worked together to cut the right size wood for our diorama. Stephen leaned in toward my dad and said, "I'm gonna need to know one thing."

"What's that?" Dad said, distracted by his measurements.

"Are you a Steelers fan or an Eagles fan?"

My dad laughed and said, "Well, you know Mrs. Brown and I are from Philly, so I admit I'm an Eagles fan. Fly, Eagles, Fly!"

"Noooooo," Stephen said and put his palm against his forehead. And then, with a serious tone, added, "Aren't you so depressed all the time? They're *terrible*."

"I can respect that." My dad held up the cut wood to show me. "Elita can choose her own allegiances. We haven't forced our football opinions on her yet."

Stephen ran over to me. "She's a Steelers fan," he announced.

"I honestly know nothing about football," I said. My stomach fluttered.

"I will teach you, young Skywalker," he said in a deep voice.

"Star Wars fan?" Dad chimed in.

"Of course!"

"I've never even seen one movie!" I admitted. "You guys can talk about Star Wars, but I have stuff to do. I have to finish my data charts for our presentation."

Stephen stepped back in actual astonishment. "Elita, if we're going to be friends, you're going to have to start taking notes on football and Star Wars." He put his finger in the air to imitate Mrs. Crisp. "Take good notes!" he shrilled.

My dad positioned a large folding table on the porch, and on top, the piece of wood as the base for our diorama. Stephen and Dad did all the math to make things "to scale" like how far the row of trees should be from where we would place a replica of my house. They also talked about how tall the trees should be so our house—and the fox—wouldn't look so tiny. I sat on the porch as we started to hot glue trees and fake little bushes to make our forest. Mrs. Rackley had purchased realistic grass and even a special blue glue that we could use to make Spring Creek.

We used rocks to build up the land so it looked like a ravine with the creek below.

At 5:22, the fox trotted past us two minutes early. I recorded the date, time, and weather; tomorrow, I'd find the sunset time from the weather website. On this night, Stephen wanted to see if the fox would travel back with some kind of rodent in his mouth. "Okay—let's set up our chairs in an hour or so. We might need a flashlight," I said. "And we'll listen for the sound of his paws."

Sometimes Stephen would hum while he worked. I kept looking at him, till he glanced up. I was embarrassed and my mouth suddenly felt dry. I coughed to clear my throat.

"Are you okay? Do you need water?" he asked.

"No. I'm . . . I'm fine." My face was still hot. "Hey, did you hear what happened at lunch?" I told him about how the teachers all gathered during lunch to admire our project and how Mrs. Harlow asked to see pictures.

"Well, it *is* the *best* project."

"I've been eating lunch in there," I said. Then I pretended to untangle the hot glue gun cord.

"I know," he said absently.

I took a deep breath and asked. "Where do *you* eat lunch?"

He kept working and didn't even look up from gluing another fern in place. "The counselor's office," he said matter-of-factly.

That surprised me. "Did you get in trouble or something?"

"Nah." He took his hat off and scratched his head. "My parents make me go to talk about my feelings. You know, my tender, precious feelings." He clutched his heart dramatically and leaned back in his chair, pretending to faint.

"Oh. Sorry. That sounds terrible."

"It's not bad. It's mostly because of my ankle, and then my mom got sick, and then the whole party thing."

"What party thing? And what happened to your mom?"

"So many questions."

"Sorry."

"Long story short, I—wait a sec—can you keep a secret? I mean seriously, EB."

"I think I can. I mean, I don't know. I hope I can." I frowned. "I can."

He laughed and swatted my arm. "You are so serious sometimes. You're like at war with yourself."

At war with myself? That's probably true.

"I'll start with the party. The party is the Fourth of July party that Justin threw. Kee was there. Anyway, it was this huge party, and some older kids were there—Justin's brothers, and they had all sorts of bad stuff there. Anyway, Justin's parents weren't there because they went camping that weekend, but they came home early because his mom had this terrible migraine or something. Before they get to the house, the cops arrive because a neighbor called them from all the noise. So Justin's mom comes home to this big party with all these illegal things, and cops actually taking down the names of kids—stuff that could be on their permanent record—and then she not only sends everyone home, but she called every parent on the soccer team to tell them."

"Oh." I didn't know what to say. "That's bad." I remembered something Mrs. Burgley had said one afternoon. She said that her motto was "Every rejection is God's protection." I hadn't been invited to that party. Was God protecting me?

"My parents freaked out. They gave me this whole speech about what kind of man I would become and how disappointed they were and how I had to quit the team because these boys were bad influences. I actually agreed with them. I mean they all used bad words and were starting to do all these bad things, right?"

"Right."

"And part of me wanted to get away from it all, right?"

"Right."

"But I didn't want to lose all my friends—you know that crowd."

"The popular crowd," I said.

"Yeah. So I faked a sprained ankle to get out of the summer soccer clinic. And then I lied and told the coach my injury was too great to play this fall. But it wasn't true. And then the guys just ignored me—they totally ghosted me, icing me out of everything. No texts, no invites, no parties. Some blocked me on my socials."

"That's hard. That's how I felt with Kee and Margo," I blurted out. I didn't want to talk about it, so I quickly asked, "But what about your mom?"

"Oh, well, she had this surgery—they thought it was cancer, but it wasn't—in August, and my dad needed all this help with my brothers and sisters. So with all that, I was just super bummed out like *all the time.* My stomach hurt, you know? And I just wanted to stay in my bed all day." He paused and went on. "Then September came, and I wasn't myself, I guess. I couldn't sit with the guys at lunch—they totally ignored me—and I couldn't go to soccer practice anymore, and I was worried about my mom recovering. It was all super heavy. So now I go to the counselor to talk about it. I know it sounds stupid. Please don't tell anyone. Don't tell Allie. Don't tell Margo or Kee."

"I won't."

We sat in silence and stared at the diorama.

"What is it like?" I finally said. "The counselor stuff. Does it help, I mean?"

"It's not bad. She asked me what kinds of things make me really, really happy. She said to do more of those things. I told her about us and the fox. She thinks it's so cool. And good news. My dad talked to the high school soccer coach. In two years, I can try out for that team. That coach doesn't allow any kind of misbehavior. You're cut from the team if you even *attend* a party. And more good news. I like the Math Team. I'm good. I'm going to take algebra next year."

"That will be so cool. I'll come and watch you compete," I said and immediately added, "with Allie."

He smiled and kept arranging little trees.

We sat for another thirty minutes and whispered about whether the woods were haunted. He held the flashlight under his chin and said, "Bwaaahahaaa!" to scare me.

"Our fox is special, don't you think?" he suddenly said. "I like thinking of him as famous. Did you hear about the video? It's like up to a hundred thousand views. What if we get a million? Allie will get verified like Margo."

"That's insane."

"What will you do when we're famous?"

"I don't want to be famous. Allie can be famous. Margo can

be famous. I think I want a simple life. Just like this." I looked at my little house. And in that moment, it was true. I didn't want another life.

"I like that about you. You're like . . . real."

The fox didn't matter anymore. Margo didn't matter. Nothing mattered but the way it felt to look in Stephen's eyes and hear his voice tell me I was real.

CHAPTER 18

RESULTS

"Where are we with things?" Allie asked as she held up her clipboard. "Let's do the checklist. Okay. Data. Do we have at least thirty days of data?"

"Check," I said proudly. "And our first hypothesis is that weather doesn't impact the timing or path of the fox. Our second hypothesis is that the fox tells time by the sunset."

"We still have a few days before we turn it in," Stephen said. "Can we add in another test?"

"Like what?" I asked.

"Like obstacles. What will the fox do if we block his path? So we can try a log one day, my bike one day, a human one day—you know, all kinds of barriers."

"What do you think he'll do?" Allie said, holding her pencil above her clipboard. She tapped her pencil on her cheek. "I think he'll just go right around or over it, but it won't stop him."

"Me too," I said.

"Me too," Stephen said. "Let's test it. I can come tomorrow night, but weeknights are too hard."

"Plus, I work at the Burgleys'. I'll set up the obstacle before I go and then watch and record what he does on my way back."

"Cool," Allie said. "And did we ever confirm that he's actually hunting? I mean do we have proof?"

"Well, my dad said he saw the fox around 8:00 the other night when he took out the garbage. But it's not regular. How could it be? The fox can't predict what he's going to catch for dinner for his family. I can sit out on Sunday right here and watch for him. I'll see if he's carrying any prey in his mouth."

"Gross," Allie said. "That's *so gross.*"

                  ♦ ♦ ♦

Was there a table in heaven for the girl who loves foxes? When I thought about my fox, I felt special. I felt right inside. At least *that* was going well for me. And sometimes, Stephen would text me a joke or something he learned about the fox. I still didn't have the right clothes, and I still didn't have a seat at the popular table, but I knew I was smart in science, and I had the best grade in math.

Well, until our math exam came back. Mr. Rivera handed back my exam and shook his head. "What happened, Elita?" he said. The whole class could hear him.

After school, I raced up to my room and hid the exam under my bed. I cried into my pillow. *If I'm not smart, I'm not anything.* Why would Jesus even want me for His table? Right before dinner, Dad came up to find me.

"How was the math test?"

"I don't want to talk about it."

"Elita, come on. It can't be that bad. What happened?"

I rolled off my bed and dug under it to find the balled-up test where a bright red C- glared at me. "There, okay? There!" I snapped.

"Did you not study?"

"I did!"

"You're not a C minus student in math," he said sternly. "Were you trying? You don't want to start getting bad study habits. Soon you'll be in high school, and if you're going to college . . ."

High school! College? Middle school was hard enough without thinking that far ahead. "Dad! Please! Please!" I'd had enough of him being disappointed in me. "I'll study harder."

"Okay. And maybe we'll find a tutor. And maybe you should spend less time with Allie and Stephen and more time on homework."

━ ━ ━

I went to school the next day. *Wrong clothes. Wrong face. Wrong grades. Wrong, wrong, wrong.*

Stephen raced to find me as I lumbered to science class.

"Okay—so what do we have so far? It's only five days till the project is due. Thursday night, Allie and I will come right after school to finish the diorama and practice our report. What's the latest, EB?"

"He just climbed over the log and rocks, went around the bicycle and leaf pile, and tonight, we see what he does when my dad stands in the middle of the hunting trail. My dad didn't want *me* that close to the fox, I guess." My deflated voice met his eager one.

"What do you think he'll do? Do you think with a human that close that he'll turn around and go back to his den?" Stephen asked.

"He has to eat. I think he'll go into the woods and pick up the trail in another spot."

"Yeah. You're right. Hey—"

"What?" I said and sighed loudly.

"When this is all over—you know, the project and all—do you think I could still come so we can find the den? Allie said that the fox pups are always born in the spring. That would be so cool if I could see those little foxes." His eyes were so wide. I smiled when I remembered how I needed to see those owlets last summer. He needed to see those pups like I needed those owlets.

"Sure," I said, still in a depressed voice. But hope started to fill me up, like I was a balloon inside. "We can search for the den—I bet I can find it."

"I know you can, EB."

When I didn't say anything but just sighed, Stephen took a step closer to me.

"EB? Are you okay? What happened? You seem mad or sad or something. Did I do something wrong?" His brown eyes looked into mine.

I stammered, filled with sudden nerves. "I . . . I did bad on my math exam. You didn't do anything wrong." *You're the only thing right, Stephen. You're the only good thing.*

"That's the worst." He looked at me with those big eyes, and it felt like he really cared about me, like it mattered to him. "I'm sorry." He said it so gently with the corners of his mouth turning down in empathy.

Then, I don't know why, but I started to cry just like the baby I was. Stephen led me to the corner of the science room behind the illustration tables so no one could see us as they streamed into the classroom.

"Hey, it's okay. You don't have to be perfect. I can help you. Remember? I'm a math genius."

I laughed through my tears.

Then, Stephen leaned over and whispered so nobody else could hear. "Listen. Don't worry. I'm here, and you aren't alone. Everything's going to be okay. All of it."

❧ ❧ ❧

Allie arrived at science class carrying a brown grocery bag. "You guys! I know how to test if he's on a hunting trail." She put the bag on my desk and stopped to catch her breath as she waved Stephen and me over to her. I wiped my tears as Stephen led me to Allie's desk. He dropped my hand but stayed close to me. He whispered one more time: *Everything's going to be okay. All of it.*

"Fruit! Foxes absolutely love fruit. They can't resist it. If we put a pile of fruit on the trail, and he stops and eats it all or carries some back home without going on to the meadow, we know he's been out hunting. If he travels on, we know he's going somewhere else—maybe building a den past the meadow—I don't know!"

Stephen and I dug into the grocery bag to find two containers of blackberries and a bag of apples.

"I know you work tonight at the Burgleys', but could Stephen and I come by to test our theory?"

"I'll see if I can leave early. I'll meet you in my backyard at 5:00."

* * *

We huddled together on the porch, waiting. We piled up apples and all the blackberries right on the trail. Even my mom and dad came out to see what would happen. We weren't surprised when Dad told us the fox just stopped and went around him as he blocked the trail, but nobody could predict what would happen with our fruit experiment. Allie turned her phone camera on. Her fox videos had over 175,000 views now, and even Margo and Kee asked about it.

"He's already here," Stephen whispered. "He must have smelled the berries and came early. Look!" He pointed. "He's stopping to eat. He's stopping!"

For almost ten minutes, the fox ate and ate—first all the blackberries, and then an apple. Then, he stuffed an apple in his mouth, turned around, and trotted home.

"We were right!" Allie said, pleased. "We were totally, 100 percent right."

CHAPTER 19

THE BIRTHDAY GIRL

On November 1, I would turn thirteen. It's a terrible birth date. I mean, everyone spends all their time and energy on Halloween, and by the time my birthday arrives the next morning, it's like an afterthought. And nobody wants *more* sugar and *more* parties. I suppose it's the same with December 26 and January 2 birthdays, too. These days feel a little sad and empty because the real celebration—that has nothing to do with you—was the day before.

It's okay though, I guess, because if you want to know the truth, I don't like parties when I'm the center of attention. And I'm always worried about whether everyone else is having fun that it ends up not being as fun as I imagined it would be. I wasn't like Margo, who could flit around a house full of people and have the time of her life. When I was little, I'd just go to a nice restaurant with my family and open a few gifts. One year, I invited Margo and Kee to a sleepover in a tent my dad put up in the backyard. Margo hated it, and Kee was scared of spiders and bears, so they both got picked up and left by 10:00, even after I said we could sleep inside. That year, Cally and Mom ended up sleeping in the tent with me, and Dad delivered a plate of bacon and pancakes right inside the tent the next morning.

Some kids dream of their thirteenth birthday. Like it's such a big deal to finally become a teenager. Like life would really begin on that day or something. Maybe, for some people, it does. I just wanted to forget about my birthday this year. Besides, it was on a Saturday, so nobody at school would even have to know or even think about me.

My mom had another idea. She broke the news in a matter-of-fact way that sent me running up to my bedroom in tears. We had been sitting together after dinner on Monday night cutting out felt ovals in grey, brown, and black. Cally was working on a spelling sheet and Dad was in the bathroom fixing our leaky faucet. Mom and I hot-glued rows and rows of ovals on a brown T-shirt to make what looked like the body of an owl. "The owl face makeup is what will really make the outfit come together," my mom explained. She always dressed up in an elaborate costume on Halloween. Cally decided to dress up as a peacock, but she'd go trick-or-treating with some school friends in town since nobody came up this far near the woods to the few spread-apart homes.

"Since Allie and Stephen will come Saturday night for the fox project, I called their parents to see about having a cookout and little birthday party for you—just the three of you since they'd already be here."

"You what?" I shouted. I banged my fist on the table. Cally looked up, interested in my rant.

"Elita—it's just dinner and cake."

"Mom—that's so awful—my mom begging my school partners to celebrate my birthday with me?"

"They seemed excited. Stephen's mom already picked out a present for him to give you, and Mrs. Wu wants to send cupcakes."

"Mom, no—Stephen being forced to bring me a present— Mom, this is so awkward. No!"

"What do you want me to do? I can't cancel."

"Why didn't you ask *me* what I wanted for my thirteenth birthday? What about going to a nice restaurant? What about something simple? I don't want a party—especially not with a boy." My face felt like fire, and tears filled my eyes. "You ruin everything, Mom! Everything!" I ran up the stairs and slammed the door to my room.

I grabbed my phone. I needed to call someone, but who? I couldn't call Margo. I couldn't call Kee. I wiped my face as I held the phone up to see I had two unread text messages. Nobody *ever* texted me—mostly because they know I never check my phone.

"Thx for the party invite!!!" I had to smile. Allie liked to use a ton of exclamation points.

"Hey."

"Hey! Did the fox come tonight?!!!!!"

"5:22. I'll compare it to sunset tomorrow."

"Do you like chocolate, vanilla, strawberry, lemon, or coconut? My mom is asking."

"Hmmm. Lemon."

"K. Bye! Gotta run. Check out our videos. 280K. We are famous!!!!!!!"

The second text was from Stephen. My heart started beating faster.

"Did u ask the fox if he was ok with a party?"

"Yeah. He's cool," I texted back.

"Can I wear normal clothes? My mom wants to know."

"Yeah. Jeans. Hoodie. Ball cap. Your usual."

"K. Good. I'm excited. Love cupcakes."

"Hope u like lemon."

"Hate lemon."

"Too bad."

"How are we even friends?"

I laughed imagining Stephen's palm on his forehead, complaining about my love of all things lemon.

I didn't know what to text next. I didn't want to say goodbye, ever. Then he wrote, "See u in Nature Club. Bye!"

* * *

On Friday, a gift bag sat in front of my locker with a big yellow balloon tied to it. Fluffs of yellow tissue paper erupted from the bag, and I could already see gold confetti all around the bag. *Margo.* This looked like Margo's work.

A sketch pad and watercolor pencils—the expensive kind I'd always wanted—and a journal with a red fox on it. The card said, "Happy 13th Birthday! Love, Margo, Lindsay, and Keanna."

Lindsay? But she *hated* me. Was this a joke? I looked again at the card. Lindsay had replaced me in what used to be my group of three: Margo, Kee, and me. Now, it was Margo, Lindsay, and Kee. I frowned and took a deep breath.

* * *

Saturday morning, Cally pounced on my bed and handed me a present she wrapped herself.

"It's really from all of us," she said with a giggle.

I unwrapped the paper that had way too much tape everywhere. I gasped.

"A Polaroid camera? Are you kidding me? Cally, this is awesome!"

"You can take pictures of stuff in the woods and of your friends and stuff."

Later that afternoon, Mom came to find me in my bedroom. She'd been prepping food for the party she'd planned for me with all my favorites: crockpot mac-n-cheese, burgers stuffed with cheese and bacon for the grill, and a fruit salad with blackberries and raspberries. I was still annoyed with her. She apologized again, and I muttered, "It's fine." She said she wanted to go shopping for a new outfit for my birthday, but I said, "I have too much homework."

* * *

We sat around a crackling fire. The air was cold and crisp, but Mom brought blankets for us. Allie handed me a box and cried,

"Open it! Open it! Open it!" and I remembered why she had that nickname Bulldog Allie.

"These are the best!" I said as I pulled out three pair of socks, each with different red fox designs on them.

"They're long, too, so you can see them over your winter boots."

"Thank you, Allie. So awesome."

"Okay, mine now," Stephen said and handed me a beautifully wrapped box—obviously something his mother put together. Inside, I found two smaller boxes with gold bows.

Inside the first box, I found a tiny glass fox figurine.

"It's perfect for the diorama, but you can keep it afterward. I found it at the craft store when my mom and I bought the little trees and hot glue." He paused and looked down as I held up the second. "Um, and that one is from my mom." He looked away, knelt down to find a stick, and started breaking it apart and throwing the pieces across the yard. Then, he gathered up the wrapping paper to stuff it into the fire.

I looked into the little box. A gold necklace with a perfect little gold fox charm. I sucked in my breath. The necklace looked like the one I imagined myself wearing in my vision of being seated on my royal throne.

"Ooooooh, put it on. It's so beautiful," Allie said while I blushed. *Jewelry from a boy. Special. Terrifying.*

"Do you think we overdid the fox theme?" Stephen said, finally looking at me.

"Maybe just a little," I said. "But we owe a lot to the fox if you think about it. I mean, we have the best project in the whole seventh grade." Allie came around my back, pulled my hair up, and helped me put on the gold fox necklace.

CHAPTER 20

POPULAR

Allie told a few people that Stephen bought me a necklace for my birthday, and word spread that I was his *girlfriend*. In homeroom, a few girls came by my desk and said, "Nice necklace," and started giggling with their hands over their mouths. "Is it true that Stephen Rackley likes you? And we heard about your video. That's so great, EB."

Lindsay asked to see the necklace in Nature Club, but her eyes didn't look kind. She looked away and walked down the trail with the other boys in the group while Stephen stayed back with me on the trail. Mr. Dale insisted the fox videos could reach a million views. Every once in a while, Lindsay would look back over her shoulder and glare at me. I walked slower and picked up a few acorns to distance myself. Stephen stayed right beside me.

"I heard everyone thinks you're my girlfriend."

"Yeah," I said.

"Is that bad?" he asked.

"I don't know," I said, blushing and stumbling as I stammered, "I have to go!"

❧ ❧ ❧

All week, I had left the Burgleys' early after talking Mrs. Burgley's ear off about my fox. We moved from the library to her sewing room to box up the fabric for her quilting. She also had several bolts of fabric against the wall in all kinds of colors.

"I won't need those," she explained. "But at one time in my life, I was quite a seamstress. I made window drapes and bedspreads. One year I made a wedding dress. Never again. The bride wanted beading and the tackiest lace I've ever seen. Gobs and gobs of it." Mrs. Burgley acted horrified, and I laughed at her. That day, I carried fabric to the truck and a whole box of spools of thread. Then I swept the floor of the sewing room.

"You're a hard worker, Elita. I admire that. I'll be sad when you won't need me anymore—I mean, uh, when we don't need you anymore."

"I'll just have to visit South Carolina," I promised.

She put her hands on her hips and shook her head. "It's hard packing up your life. Lots of memories in this house."

We stopped working for snack time at 4:30—herbal tea and cookies frosted to look like jack-o'-lanterns. I knew she picked them up from the grocery store just for me.

"I've been praying for you," she said as we munched on our cookies. "I remembered one more thing I wanted to tell you about my seventh grade year."

"Something more about my seat with Jesus?" I said, reminding her in case she was going to pull out Ephesians and tell me the same story again as older people sometimes do.

"It's related." She sipped her tea. "It's something I took too long to do."

"What?"

"Forgive them."

"Who?"

"The popular girls. I think forgiveness is the most powerful force in the universe. It is if you stop and think about it."

I tilted my head up to the ceiling to think. I tried to imagine forgiving Margo for ruining my seventh grade year, but I suddenly realized that she didn't *intend* to hurt me. She was just Margo, after all. She was just being herself all those times. "I think maybe I've already forgiven Margo, Mrs. Burgley." *But Lindsay? Ugh.*

"I think you have, too," she said and handed me the box of cookies. "Take all of them. You'll need some for your fox group and your sister. Yes, take them all. There's plenty."

CHAPTER 21

THE CRIME

On Friday morning, my dad dropped off the diorama to Mr. Dale's class for our presentation. Allie's mom made the whole class sugar cookies iced with fox designs. My knees bounced from excitement in every period as I waited for science class. Allie would summarize our research on foxes, Stephen would explain our diorama and the trail of the fox, and I'd show a graph of our data that included the times, the weather, the sunset times, and the week we tested if obstacles would disturb the hunting pattern. We would prove that the fox tells time by the setting sun. And the best part of all was how Mr. Dale announced a reporter from the *Daily Times* was coming to interview us for the newspaper.

In Nature Club, I saw that Stephen had dressed up with a nice shirt and bowtie with little foxes on it. "We've all gone fox crazy, EB," he said.

That day in Nature Club, we were supposed to look for

evidence of hibernating frogs and snakes under fallen logs and piles of leaves on the forest floor. Mr. Dale gave us each a partner, and we'd go into the woods and work together to carefully lift up logs to see what was underneath. He paired me with Lindsay. She crossed her arms and rolled her eyes.

We walked in silence along the trail as partners peeled off to find fallen trees. "Let's go down near the edge of the ravine," I said. "Near the creek. I bet we'll find frogs and salamanders under the leaves there."

"Whatever."

"But I don't want to get too dirty—I have our fox presentation next period," I mentioned. "And Mrs. Harlow is bringing the whole eighth grade science class."

"Would you stop talking about that fox? That's all you talk about—that stupid fox. You know people think it's weird, right? Check the comments. People think you guys are freaks."

"I don't care," I said as I walked closer to the creek. *Why did she have to be so mean? What did I ever do to her?*

"Stephen and Allie don't think it's weird," I finally said.

"You know they just used you to get the grade. And you know what I think is so funny about your fox project?" Lindsay said and grabbed my arm to make me stop walking. She squeezed it hard. I looked around. I couldn't see anyone else, and Mr. Dale was far away by the school. My heart pounded. She squeezed harder.

"What's so funny—what's seriously hilarious—is that all your research just helps hunters kill foxes better, right? I mean you can track their patterns and kill them better. They'll lay traps on their hunting trails." She glared at me as I shook my arm free from her grasp. "It's like your project should really be called *How to Murder Foxes Better*."

She tried to grab my arm again as she said, "Plus, you're so annoying."

"Stop it," I said. "Let go of my arm. You're crazy. You're mean. Why do you hate me so much?"

"Fox killer," she taunted.

I thought she would lunge for me, hit me, or push me down the ravine. I dug my nails into her hand that held my arm and then shoved her away so that she fell down. My nails made bright drops of blood form on her arm. "Leave me alone," I yelled. I saw her stand up and brush the leaves off her jeans as I ran as fast as I could back to the school.

• • •

"Elita Brown, please come to the principal's office." We had finished our fox presentation, and the class had cheered as they ate Allie's cookies. Mr. Dale said he wanted to submit our project as a display for Penn State's Environmental Center. Stephen gave us each a high five. The newspaper took pictures and interviewed Allie as our spokesperson. Lindsay never even showed up for science class.

I gathered my books and wondered if Principal Markham would give me an award. Maybe *National Geographic* was waiting to offer me a job. I smiled as I walked down the empty hallway past rows of lockers and corny motivational posters that said things like BE YOURSELF. *I was myself. I was one hundred percent*

myself with my fox project and with Stephen and Allie.

I entered the office and froze. My dad was there. He should have been at work at that time of the day. He frowned at me and shook his head. He pointed to Mr. Markham's door and told me to go in and take a seat. When I walked in, the principal stood up. I sat down and then saw that to my right, sitting on a long brown couch, were Lindsay Myers and her father.

Lindsay was covered in blood that seeped through bandages the nurse must have just applied. She had a gash on her arm and another on her cheek. Her hair was tangled and filled with leaves and dirt from the woods. Her T-shirt was torn at the collar.

Principal Markham turned to me and said, "We will not accept bullying, fighting, or malice at this school, Elita. I'm so disappointed and quite frankly shocked. You're one of the best students in our school." He let that sink in and continued. "I'm not sure what the Myers family will choose to do, but if they file a police report about this, juvenile assault isn't a joke, Elita. People go to detention centers for this, even at your age."

"Assault?" I stammered.

"Lindsay told us about what happened in the woods. She says you got upset because she made fun of your fox project. Is that right? Were you upset about your fox?"

"I was upset." I looked back and forth from my dad to the principal.

"Did you shove Lindsay so she fell down? She said you clawed your nails into her. That you caused her to bleed, right?"

"Yes," I said, and then I burst into tears. "But then I came right back to school. I didn't mean to hurt her. I was trying to—"

"Elita, I think you've become a little obsessed with your fox. Lindsay says you lost control in the woods, tried to push her down the ravine, and that you proceeded to throw rocks at her until she bled. You were stoning her. She could have died, Elita."

"No," I tried to say but I was crying so hard I couldn't speak anymore. "That's not true. That's not what happened."

"That's enough," my dad said softly. "I'm taking Elita home."

"For now, she'll have a one-week suspension. And we'll move Elita out of her elective and science class to have a different schedule from Lindsay."

"Suspension? I'm asking for *expulsion*. Look at what she's done to my girl!" Mr. Myers said and glared at me.

My dad placed his hand firmly on my shoulder and walked me to our car. He kept shaking his head and said, "I just don't understand." When we arrived home, I finally said, "Dad, she's lying. I was mad, and I *did* shove her down, but she grabbed my arm—hard—like she was going to hurt me. I was defending myself. And I never pushed her down the ravine. And I never threw rocks at her. She is a liar. She hates me."

"Elita. Go to your room. I'm taking your phone away, and I want you to stay in your room until your mom and I tell you to come out. I knew you'd become too focused on that fox. And the way you treated your mother before your birthday party—"

"But I work at the Burgley house after school," I interrupted.

"Not today. I'll call Irvin and tell him. And I'll ask Shirley to pray. I don't know what happened to you, Elita. You've become a different person ever since you started seventh grade."

I burst into fresh tears and ran up the stairs to my room.

CHAPTER 22

THE TRAP

I burrowed into my pillow. I was like a fox in a steel trap, hopeless, where any movement on my part would only make the situation worse. *Suspended. Maybe I'd even be arrested or go to jail.* I could hear my mom and dad downstairs arguing about me. I could hear Cally ask what I did and how long I'd be in trouble for.

I was shaking and crying and sadder than I'd ever been in my whole life. Could my life get worse? Kids at school would hate me. My parents hated me. My teachers would hate me. Even the Burgleys would hate me when they heard that I pushed Lindsay down a ravine and threw rocks at her. They'd believe the Myers family. Now I could add a bad reputation to my list of all the reasons I'd never have a seat at the table I wanted.

And Mrs. Burgley had tried so hard to tell me I was seated at some special table with Jesus. Where was God now? If God loved me, why would He let these last three months be the worst ever?

The high-top tables. My clothes. Margo's face when she opened her poodle birthday present. My C- on my math exam. Lindsay Myers. And now my whole life was ruined forever.

God, what is happening? I pulled my burgundy Bible off the shelf. I closed my eyes and whispered into the thin air for God to hear me and *help me*.

Mrs. Burgley said God spoke to her through the Bible. She said that God was her *present help in time of need*. I needed help, but I didn't know where to start reading my Bible. It was a bulky, confusing, and weird book. I opened it up, right to the very middle, where all the poems called psalms were. Some guy named David—the same one who beat that giant Goliath—was writing about his enemy that lied about him, too. I felt like I could understand that. I kept reading. How was it possible that it felt like I was reading about my own life in that old book?

I couldn't believe it.

David was writing things I was feeling. Is this what Mrs. Burgley meant about God speaking?

I started with Psalm 5 where David said God hears his voice. Then I read how David described his enemy, and it sounded exactly like Lindsay Myers. He said, "O God, declare them guilty. Let them be caught in their own traps."

My heart felt warm but tight. Could God see me and hear me? It seemed like it. It seemed like God was right with me. And I felt loved. I felt like Someone was teaching me. And I remembered Mrs. Crisp's advice to take good notes.

I took a pencil and underlined parts of Psalm 5. Then I flipped a few pages to more of David's poems. In Psalm 30, he said, "O Lord my God, I called to you for help, and you healed me . . . weeping may remain for a night, but rejoicing comes in the morning." I circled the words weeping and rejoiced. I whispered, "God, I need You. Please help me. I don't know what to do. Show me what to do about Lindsay. I'm trapped. God! I'm caught like a helpless fox in a steel trap."

I pictured my seat with Jesus in the heavenly realms. I pictured myself talking right to Him. He was right there next to me. On the next page of my Bible, I read David saying to God, "Free me from the trap that is set for me, for you are my refuge. Into your hands I commit my spirit; redeem me, O Lord, the God of truth."

Finally, I knew the Bible was working. I knew how to talk to God and experience Him as I read those words. *God, I cannot survive seventh grade without You anymore. I'm not sure I'm actually a Christian, but right now, I give You my heart and my whole life. You are my only hope, God. Free me from this trap like You freed David. Help me know how to tell the truth, and help people believe me. I don't know what to do.*

I knew God was speaking because what happened next could only be Jesus. In my heart, I heard the whisper of something— not like a voice, but something deeper. I heard this: *Don't worry. Pray for Lindsay Myers. Forgive Lindsay Myers.*

❧ ❧ ❧

I woke up with the Bible cracked open on my chest. I was wearing the same clothes as the day before. The morning sun peeked through my curtains, and the sunlight on the dust made my room sparkle. I wiped my eyes and looked down at my Bible. I had the strangest dream that my fox was outside my window all night with his head bowed down like he was praying. In my dream, I went outside and followed him into the silvery moonlit woods till he showed me something high in the trees. There, I saw Mrs. Burgley pointing up to the trees, too, to show me what I needed to see.

I could smell pancakes and bacon. And the weirdest thing of all is that I still felt like God was with me. I felt a strange hope inside of me. I felt impossibly happy. It was like that same feeling I had when I fell from the pine tree and how, miraculously, I was still alive even though I had a stick protruding from my arm. I had pain and joy at the same time.

It didn't matter what happened with Lindsay, with those lunchroom tables, or with anything else because I had my seat with Jesus. Then I remembered that feeling I had that I should pray for Lindsay. I whispered, "God, I'm not sure what happened to Lindsay to make her so mean. But I guess I'm asking that You help her, too." Ugh. I didn't want to pray that prayer. It was like another, better me—a reinvented me—prayed that prayer. That mean girl, the one who wanted bad things to happen to Margo, Kee, and Lindsay wasn't there anymore.

I looked out my window into the forest that sparkled with morning dew. I thought of the hunters out in the game lands who waited all night for bear and wild turkey. I thought about my fox safe in his den somewhere near my house.

I watched a hawk circling high above the pines like a guardian of the forest.

That's when I remembered what I was looking at in my dream. My eyes widened. My heart raced. I opened my mouth and started whooping and hollering, "That's it! Yes! I'm free!"

I knew exactly how God would set me free from Lindsay's trap.

"Mom! Dad!" I yelled.

I wiped my eyes. Puffy and red from tears, they stung. But God had said tears would flow in the night, but joy would come in the morning. Joy had come.

You see, I knew something about the Pennsylvania woods that Lindsay didn't know.

And you don't mess with a girl who knows the Pennsylvania woods. A naturalist. A lead scientist. Don't even try.

CHAPTER 23

THE ESCAPE

Lindsay sat with her arms crossed over her flannel shirt. We again gathered in Principal Markham's office, this time with Superintendent Wu, my parents, Lindsay's dad, and another man, husky and wearing a big brown jacket, someone I'd never seen before.

"I'll get right to it," Mr. Wu said. "Mr. Markham? Your thoughts?"

"Mr. and Mrs. Brown, Elita—" the principal looked down into whatever he was doing on his laptop. "We want to apologize to you for all you've been through and—"

"What?" Lindsay's father interrupted. "This is outrageous."

"I have here beside me Jacob Bowen from Potter's Ford, across town." Mr. Bowen raised his hand in a silent greeting as the principal went on. "He's a fireman there and a notable hunter. He serves on the Game Commission Board. He's the one who helps design the blinds you see up in the trees down in the forest when you get to the game lands. He also leads the Young Hunter's group every November and teaches firearm safety."

My knees bounced up and down and my mom put her hand on them to settle me down.

"Well, Elita remembered something she observed down by Spring Creek last summer."

I beamed. I clasped my hands together, waiting.

"The Game Commission has been tracking the wildlife down near Spring Creek. Last year, they set up motion sensor cameras in certain trees to monitor the deer and bear activity—both for hunting, but obviously for safety reasons—and for some research on elk, too. The trail cams help us know what we're dealing with."

The cameras were hidden in little lock boxes tied high up in the trees and they pointed down toward the understory. When wildlife came in view, the cameras would turn on.

"We checked the cameras, Mr. Myers. Jake here came to the office this morning with some footage his camera caught of the girls on the day Lindsay said Elita pushed her down the ravine and threw rocks at her."

I sat in silence between my parents. When I called out to my parents on Saturday, I told my dad I could prove Lindsay was lying. I remembered that near the ravine, I saw those little boxes high in the trees that recorded deer activity. Was there a chance it recorded Lindsay and me? I begged Dad to call his hunter friends and find out how to see the camera footage.

Mr. Bowen coughed and kept shifting uncomfortably in his seat. "There's no audio, just video."

Mr. Markham turned his laptop around, and we all leaned in

as he pressed play. You could see Lindsay and me come into view, and our faces looked angry. You could tell by our mouths that Lindsay was shouting at me, and then I was shouting at her.

"That's her grabbing *my* arm—that's why I had to shove her," I said and pointed at the screen. We could see Lindsay stand up and wipe the leaves and dirt off her jeans.

"I left her—when I started toward the school—but Lindsay stayed by the tree, and when I looked back, she was pacing in little circles."

"Stop it," Lindsay cried. "I don't want to watch this. Let's just drop the whole thing."

"I don't understand," Mr. Myers said. "Who attacked my daughter, then? Are you telling me a bear comes? Did some hunter come and attack her?"

Lindsay stayed still as a statue, staring blankly at the wall, her jaw clenched in anger and humiliation as the rest of us continued to watch the video. In the video, she started acting like a wild dog or something. She rolled around in the leaves and rubbed dirt on her arms and jeans. She took dark berries and rubbed them to make it look like she was bleeding. She kept rolling around until a stick cut her face and her arms were scratched up. Then she messed her hair up and tried twice to rip her T-shirt at the collar. Finally, she walked out of frame, and the camera turned off with no more motion.

"Lindsay! Why would you do that?" Her father was angry. He even said, "What's wrong with you?"

Lindsay never cried. She never moved. I looked at her face and suddenly felt this strange sorrow. I tried to imagine her life:

Where was her mother? Why did she move away from all her friends in Colorado? What made her so angry?

"You owe the Brown family, and especially Elita, an apology. You've caused a lot of pain, and we have no tolerance for bullying at this school and lying like this," Mr. Wu said. "And my daughter told me she's seen graffiti in the girls' restroom that says 'Elita has fox rabies.' Perhaps that's your doing as well? I'm sorry, but we'll need to talk privately now."

I looked at Lindsay one more time, for the last time I'd ever see her.

CHAPTER 24

AN EXPLANATION

My phone rang that night as I sat on my bed. I was staring at the wall, just thinking. I do that sometimes. Sometimes I think about the future or imagine where else I'd rather be, or I daydream about what I hope happens the next day at school. Or I think about my fox. I don't know, I just *think*. And I'll do weird things like stretch my arms high in the air or make scissor slices with my legs. And I just breathe, I guess.

"Hello," I said slowly.

"Lindsay was jealous. She heard me and the girls saying they wish they were more like Elita Brown in science class," Margo exclaimed into the phone. "I feel like this is all *my* fault."

I guess word spread. I bet Allie texted the whole seventh grade after I told her.

"More like me?" I sucked my breath in and held it there. "Like *me*?" I learned long ago that when Margo starts talking, you just catch up to whatever she's saying.

"And one day Lindsay said that her mom loved foxes, too, but they have gray foxes in Colorado, and when we tried to ask her about her mom, she left the lunch table. And then the whole part about Stephen Rackley just upset her, and she couldn't think of a good way to handle the jealousy, I think. That's what my mom thinks, too. I mean, Lindsay was totally obsessed with Stephen."

"What part about Stephen?"

"The part where he wanted to go to the winter dance with *you*, and not her. He told Kee's boyfriend, and he told the lunch table the day before Lindsay and you were in the woods. She heard him say it."

"Oh," I said. My face felt hot, and I wanted to change the subject immediately. I started biting my thumbnail—and I don't even bite my nails. "I'm never in the lunchroom, so I didn't hear that." I wanted to ask Margo about all those days and days of never having a seat for me, about that terrible day when she said the worst three words I'd ever heard in my life—*This seat's saved*. But I couldn't. Maybe I was too happy about Stephen. Maybe I was just happy to hear Margo's voice again. Maybe Mrs. Burgley was right about how forgiveness is the greatest thing in the entire world.

"So will you go?"

"Go where?"

"To the dance! The dance! And will you please let me do your hair and makeup? My word, Elita, you still look like you did in the fourth grade. And don't buy a dress—'cause I know you won't anyway—I've got like fifteen dresses here that you can choose from." Her words felt kind, not like she was shaming me. "And I want to interview you for my TikTok. Your fox project has like 750,000 views."

"Okay," I said. "That's fine. And I know I look like a little kid. My mom says I'm a late bloomer. I think I do need help!" We both laughed.

Before I put down the phone, Margo said: "And I learned something. Allie had overheard her father say Lindsay's mom walked out on them and Mr. Myers came to Pennsylvania to start a new life. The school said they'd support Lindsay however she needed, but Mr. Myers said he was pulling Lindsay out of our school and sending her to a private one."

＊＊＊

There's this part in the Bible where God says He can do im-measurably more than we ask or imagine. I love that word: *im-measurably*. And I had the weirdest thought as I hung up the phone with Margo. I thought about all those times I controlled every play date when we were little. I always forced her to do things in the woods, and she never really liked it. She tolerated it. What she really loved was fashion and makeup and all the glamorous things that I absolutely detested. Did I even want to sit at the popular table? Did Margo realize that I'd be miserable there? At her birthday party, if she had invited me to do hair and makeup beforehand, it would have felt like torture to me. Maybe people grow apart in seventh grade because you figure out who you really are and what you want. Some girls will sit at the popular table. Some won't. I didn't, and I never would. And now I was thinking, for the first time in my life, that this was okay. It wouldn't make me happy because it wasn't *me*.

◢ ◢ ◢

"I'm glad the whole Lindsay thing happened to you," Stephen said, as he pelted me with marshmallows across the fire pit. The ones I didn't catch in my mouth I directed into the fire where we watched them ooze and grow like giant molten snakes. He still came over on Saturdays to watch for the fox. He had his own routines just like our fox—he loved watching for him.

"Okay, that's mean. That's rude," I said as I caught a marshmallow and aimed it at his face.

"No, I'm serious. Think about it." He sat up straight like he was addressing a jury. "Imagine: Your kid comes home from seventh grade after having a really bad day—like a bad grade or like nobody pays attention to her in drama club or something, right—and you can actually say, 'You haven't had a bad day in seventh grade until the new girl frames you for assault in the forest and you almost get expelled.'" He started laughing hysterically while saying, "Your kids can't complain about *anything*, ever."

Everyone had said that Stephen would ask me to the winter dance, but he never had. We had been alone together plenty of times, too—in Nature Club, at my house, in the hallways at school. Nothing. Nada. No mention of the dance.

Allie already had a date—Rinaldo from the Math Team. It

wasn't Cole Enlow, but at least Rinaldo was cute and really funny. *Maybe on Monday, I'll ask Allie to tell Rinaldo to tell Stephen to ask me. Or I could just text her tonight.*

"EB?"

"What?"

"Did you hear me?"

"Sorry! I was thinking about something else," I said.

"I asked if you heard about Allie and Rinaldo."

"Oh, you mean the winter dance? Yeah, she told me."

"Do you want to kinda go with me?" Just like that. Simple. To the point. "I mean, the fox bowtie will be making an appearance. And Allie's mom wants to have us for dinner before the dance. A bunch of kids from the Math Team are coming. It's a great group. So we'd meet up there and then her dad'll drive us to the dance. Please say yes."

I smiled. My mom would let me go to the dance with a group for sure!

"Yes. And of course we need the fox bowtie. I'll get a dress to match."

CHAPTER 25

THE HIGH-TOP TABLES

I walked into the lunchroom for the first time in three months. I saw Margo sitting alone at the high-top tables as she waited for her friends to come through the lunch line. It was fried chicken sandwiches and French fries, so the line was longer than usual. I walked peacefully over to her like my whole world hadn't imploded since she said those terrible words to me on the first day of school.

"Hey, Margo."

"Hey, EB. I just love that everyone calls you EB. It's so cute." She was drawing a dress design in her sketch book.

"That's pretty," I said.

"Sit down. I'll show you my best ones."

Sit down.

Was it that easy? Here I am at the high-top tables, sitting where I'd wanted to sit for months. I had been fighting for a seat here, and now here I am.

163

She flipped through her sketch book as I dumped my lunch sack on the table.

"Stephen asked me to the dance," I said.

She pretended her whole body was frozen as she exaggerated her words with big eyes, her hands frozen by her face. "I knew it. Stephen Rackley is so gorgeous." Then, like a spell had been broken, Margo erupted into squeals and the Margo clap. "Okay, so the dress. What's the dress situation?"

Her friends started to gather around us and take their seats. Everyone turned to listen to me. "I thought I'd get my friend Mrs. Burgley to sew me one."

"Like one you design yourself?" Margo asked. "Genius." Then she turned to the girls and said, "Ladies, we have a job. Due tomorrow. Elita's perfect Winter Dance Gown. Oh, let us, Elita."

All the girls chimed in, "Please let us! Let us design your dress. We've been working so hard in Fashion Design. Please let us!"

For the rest of the lunch period, they asked all about Stephen. They asked to see the necklace. They talked about how I'd wear my hair and what makeup I might choose. For the first time in my whole life, I felt *popular*. Everyone talked to *me*. Everyone wanted my attention.

But I looked out over the lunchroom, and I saw Allie laughing with Rinaldo and the kids from the Math Team. I saw some of the Nature Club students with their Field Notes notebooks. They were looking over the worksheet Mr. Dale gave us on tree sicknesses of Pennsylvania. I could no longer hear what Margo and the girls were saying. I didn't want to be at Margo's table anymore. I wanted to be where people were talking about *blight* and *apple scab* and *verticillium wilt*.

✎ ✎ ✎

At my locker the next morning, Margo stood clutching her sketch book. When she saw me, she raced over and said, "It's perfect. It's absolutely darling. My girls thought of a gold full-length skirt with a bright red lining—perfect for Christmas. Huge bow at the back, see? And the bodice—that's what you call the top part—is gold velvet trimmed with the same red that will peek out from under your skirt when you're dancing or twirling. It's like a fancy T-shirt on top—comfy but so, so fancy."

"Thanks!" I said. "I'll see what Mrs. Burgley can do with this design."

"Or look at these." She held up her phone where she had taken a photo of a bunch of dresses fanned out on her bed. "You can always choose one of these."

I zoomed in on the photo to look at all of Margo's dresses. But what caught my eye was her pillow. Right there resting on Margo's pillow was the purple poodle I bought her for her birthday. She did love it, after all.

CHAPTER 26

THE DRESS

Mrs. Burgley gasped when I showed her. "I'm horrified. Does Margo want you to look like a giant metallic statue? No, no, no. I do like the color scheme, but let's try a muted, less shiny gold with layers that sort of fluff out so you can truly see the red underneath. It will look like autumn leaves descending. And we'll make it fall at the knee—much nicer for someone your age. I talked to your mother, and she agrees with me." She made some marks on the sketch with her pencil. "And how about two simple red straps? In fact, when you spin, we could actually have some other autumn colors. This is perfect for your skin tone, Elita."

She pulled out her measuring tape.

The dress only took a few days because Mrs. Burgley worked every day and most evenings to finish it. My dress was wrapped in tissue paper and sitting on her kitchen table when I arrived on Saturday morning. I carefully unwrapped it and held it up in front of me. Folds of autumn colors danced as she shook the dress on the hanger. "It's a tribute to autumn but a welcoming of winter with the gold and red. And I do believe you've grown since September."

"Really?" I didn't even blush. I said, "I love it. I really, really love it!"

Later, we sat in her bedroom to sort clothing. She wanted me to pack some of her winter clothes to give away since she wouldn't need as many of them in South Carolina. "I've had some of these sweaters for sixty years. Time does fly."

"You have a beautiful wardrobe," I said as I looked at the carefully folded sweaters, slacks, and rows of shoes to go with her church dresses.

"I used to worry so much about my appearance. I spent a fortune on face creams and makeup and all the right clothes. But that all changed."

"What happened?"

"You know—being seated at the table with Jesus. I was already at the table with the beautiful people who knew Jesus, and I could just radiate His love through my face. There's even a Bible verse about that in the Psalms. It says, 'Those who look to him are radiant; their faces are never covered with shame.' I didn't have to be beautiful anymore. I could be *radiant*. When you are seated with Christ, you radiate beauty."

I looked at her wrinkled skin—so papery and thin it reminded me of onion skin—and realized how loving and radiant her face was. I loved looking at her soft eyes. She did radiate. Could I radiate one day?

"And I used to worry about being rich all the time. But look out there," she said and pointed to the forest outside her bedroom window. "You never have to worry about being rich because you have the riches of nature always available to you."

"I do know that." I pictured all the things I loved in nature that cost me nothing to observe—the turtles, the owls, the deer, the fox.

She paused and then her eyes looked sad.

"Elita—we already have an offer on the house. A young couple with a new baby. We're moving in just a week or two. We won't need your help after today."

"Oh." I felt oddly empty.

"I have loved talking to you and sharing my life with you."

"Me too."

"Before you leave, I want to share my favorite quote with you. Maybe you could write it down to keep in your locker or in your backpack, so you don't forget. Here it is. Are you ready?"

"I'm ready."

"All seats provide equal viewing of the universe."

I didn't get it. "Huh?"

"Okay—listen carefully. It's a quote from the museum guide of the Hayden Planetarium in New York City. Do you know what a planetarium is? It's that dark theater where you look up and can see all the stars and planets and constellations."

"Yes!" I said, "I have been to a planetarium—when our fifth

grade class went to the Penn State one!"

"Do you remember how you could sit anywhere and not miss any part of the show? Well, the museum guide told me that the first time school children visit the planetarium, they all race to the very front row to get the best seat in an arena. But actually, there are no best seats. So the guide has to call out, 'Children, all seats provide equal viewing of the universe. No matter where you sit, you won't miss any part of the show.'" She paused to see if I understood.

Mrs. Burgley continued. "Elita, that's what our seat with Jesus is like. No matter where we sit in our life—no matter what kind of life He gives us—we won't miss any part of the love, joy, peace, and purpose He has for us. No matter where we sit, we won't miss out on anything He has planned for us. You don't have to be jealous. You don't have to be ashamed of your body, your clothes, your grades. Doesn't that make your heart warm?"

I nodded. I understood.

I had thought I had missed out on all the good things in life because I wasn't popular. But Mrs. Burgley taught me that, with Jesus in my life, I won't miss out on anything I'm supposed to have. And in every place I find myself, I have all sorts of blessings and good things right there. I liked this whole new life where I could be seated with Jesus every day. *All seats provide equal viewing of the universe.*

CHAPTER 27

THE NEW ME

I loved my new bedtime routine. I'd wash my face, brush my teeth, put on my pajamas, and then get under my covers to read the Psalms. Sometimes, I just reread Ephesians 2. Maybe God would keep speaking to me. I could return to Him every night at this same time—like a fox on the hunting trail—to find Him watching and waiting for me. I could follow Him down new trails.

Sometimes I also flip back through my Field Notes journal. I love looking at all the new vocabulary words and the charts I made in October.

I found that first word: *understory*. It was a funny word to call the forest floor. Like a story happening underneath the top story. It felt like a way to think about seventh grade. I mean, for me, I was just living my boring seventh grade life with this top story of the lunchroom rejection, my fox, and the Burgleys. But the whole time, there was another story happening underneath what I could see. There was a story of God loving me and inviting me to my seat with Jesus—the understory. And even though the understory of a forest feels dark and sad and scary at first, it's where all the secrets of the forest are—the beautiful ferns and all the nourishment for those tall trees. I was like a forest: I had two layers to me. I had my life in Pennsylvania in these woods and my *spiritual* life.

I think Mrs. Burgley would be proud that my brain was growing to understand things beneath the surface. Just as I was growing physically, I needed to grow up in my own soul.

The other day, I asked my mom if she wanted to walk down to the creek with me. She had made some lemonade and popcorn for our after-school snack. Cally wouldn't come home from dance for another hour. I had jammed another handful of popcorn in my mouth when I asked my mom about walking with me, and she said, "You know, you could eat more properly now that you're thirteen years old. More like a lady?"

"Mom—" I said slowly and took a deep breath. "Every conversation we have is about you improving me."

She looked at me as she put her hiking boots on. "I guess that's true. Elita, I'm so sorry I push you so hard."

We walked out to the woods, and by habit, I scanned the woods for my fox.

"Do you miss the Burgleys?" Mom asked.

"Yeah. Mrs. Burgley taught me a lot." I paused. "Mom? Did you ever think it was weird that I loved nature so much and that I wasn't growing up as fast as Margo or Kee? I mean, did I seem weird to you?"

"Never. You seemed perfect to me. But they really changed this year, and sometimes I think they're trying to grow up too fast. You don't have to do everything in middle school—save something for when you're older. There's lots to look forward to. And anyway, you're changing in your own way. And that's the most important—being true to yourself. You actually seem happy again."

"It's been a terrible few months until recently." I paused again. "Mom—I didn't know where to sit in the lunchroom. Margo and Kee—they didn't save a seat for me. It was terrible. Like I didn't belong anywhere."

I couldn't look at her. I started to cry. My mom hugged me, and I let her.

"Elita, I had a Margo and Kee. I remember the middle school lunchroom."

That's when I told her everything Mrs. Burgley had taught me: the secret you don't keep but tell. For the first time, I opened up my heart to my mom. I don't know why I waited so long. I walked beside Mom and wiped my tears away. I thought how Jesus had given me the best seat. He gave me the woods and the creek. He gave me a fox. He gave me a family and a house where spaghetti dinner was sometimes waiting for me. He gave me Stephen and Allie. He gave me a dad who showed his best love by keeping me in budget and a little sister who brought so much fun into my life. And most of all, Jesus gave me the Burgleys and Bo and Bee.

And if I didn't have any of this, I would still have my seat with Jesus.

All this, and a seat with Jesus, too.

✦ ✦ ✦

I walked back into Siler Middle School. But this time, I didn't feel invisible. I didn't feel left out. Because I knew the truth: When you're seated with Christ, you don't need to fight for a seat at the table anymore. You can actually take your eyes off yourself and love people and include them. December meant fresh, white snow. I could start fresh and feel clean inside just like that white snow that covered everything. I forgave Margo and Kee. I could even forgive Lindsay. I could talk to my mother more and give my little sister more attention. I could stop thinking of myself all day long.

I walked into the lunchroom and considered my seat with Jesus. I was already at the best table, so now what? I sat down with Allie, Rinaldo, and Stephen, but then I looked around me. I waved to a girl from my English class who hardly spoke but who wrote the best stories. "Come sit with us," I called. "I saved a seat for you."

She smiled and practically raced to our table.

And then I saw a girl from my math class sitting alone. She carefully peeled an orange as she looked blankly ahead of her. "Hey! Hey! Come sit with us!"

She looked up and waved back. "I'm on my way!" she cried.

Then, something wonderful happened. Something supernatural. I had been asking God to bring me joy since sometimes I wanted a best friend but didn't have one. Stephen was great, and I'd love being at the dance with him and our group, but I could only talk about Star Wars and the Steelers for so long. And Allie was so busy with all her clubs. I told God that if He couldn't bring me a best friend, at least He could send me some more joy.

I saw a new girl with a Field Notes journal who wanted to join Nature Club. She wore a green camouflage T-shirt. I walked over to her. "Hey, I'm Elita Brown." We were almost the same height. She had bangs. I saw mud caked on her sneakers.

"The fox girl! I've heard about you. I'm more of a trout girl myself. We live on the other side of Siler's Ridge. My family moved here from Lancaster to work for the Game Commission."

"Do you want to sit with us?"

"Sure. I'm a packer. It's weird but I love salami sandwiches. I'm obsessed with salami." *Her signature sandwich.*

"What's your name?"

"Ugh. I hate my name. It's boring. I really need a nickname."

"Just tell me."

"My name is Joy. My parents say it's the best fruit of the Spirit. You know, from the Bible and all?"

I asked God for joy. Here Joy was. I wanted the emotion; God sent a person.

"I love trout fishing, too," I said. "Do you make your own flies?"

"Not yet, but I'm learning. Plus, the Commission just dropped the license fee. We can fish for like a couple of dollars for the whole year."

"Cool—so we're over there." I stretched my arm and pointed behind me to our table. My shirt sleeve slid up. Joy saw my scar.

"Awesome scar. How did you get it?" Joy leaned in for a closer look.

We walked to our table, and I explained about the owls and the tree.

"Eastern pine, right? The owls nest there. I can see them from my window," Joy said. "I got binoculars last year. I can show you the nest if you want. Will your parents let you come over sometime? My parents are cool, but they are super strict. They won't let me have a phone yet."

I thought about falling from that pine tree and how I told my mom it had been worth it, even with those stitches and that scar.

As I sat down next to Joy, I thought about those rules of seventh grade—you know, having the right phone and choosing the right elective and wearing the right brands. None of that mattered in the end. But so far in seventh grade, I had learned one rule that *did* matter (besides, of course, Mrs. Crisp's life rule to *take good notes*, especially if you're walking in the woods and a red fox trots in front of you).

Here's the rule you need: When you walk into the lunchroom—or any room, really—think about God. Remember the best words anyone could ever say to a seventh grade girl like me:

You're already seated at the best table with Jesus.

ABOUT THE AUTHOR

Heather Holleman is a speaker, author, and college professor. She loves helping people connect with Jesus, and her favorite Bible passage is Ephesians 2:6. When Heather was in middle school, her science project that tracked the hunting patterns of the red fox along Little Hunting Creek made it to the regional science fair. She still loves hiking and hunting for turtles in the woods behind her home and along Spring Creek in Centre County, Pennsylvania.

TO THINK ABOUT AND TALK ABOUT IN *THIS SEAT'S SAVED*

1. Elita realizes there are two middle school rules she thinks guarantee popularity: have the right phone and choose the right elective. What are some unofficial "rules" of popularity in your school?

2. Elita tells the reader her two favorite sounds are "the hooting of an owl and the way the wind sounds in the trees at night." What are two of your favorite sounds?

3. Elita has a unique *signature sandwich*—melted cheese and sliced tomato with fresh dill, while her mother likes turkey and mustard on rye. Do you have a signature sandwich?

4. In your opinion, do Margo and Kee intend to hurt Elita's feelings and exclude her? Why or why not?

5. Elita tries to define popularity after she sees Mr. Dale's poster on hypotheses. How would you define popularity, and why was it so important to Elita?

6. Elita feels most like herself when she's in the woods. Where do you feel most like yourself?

7. Elita often talks about things that give her "cozy feelings" or put her in a "cozy mood." What causes you to feel "cozy"?

8. Do you have a favorite teacher you admire like Mr. Dale Robinson, Mrs. Crisp, or Mrs. Harlow?

9. Stephen and Allie love the Math Team, and other students love Nature Club or the Fashion Design elective. What is your ideal club to join?

10. Why do you think Stephen doesn't want anyone to know he goes to see the school counselor?

11. What do you think would have helped Lindsay Myers with her jealousy?

12. Did Elita do the right thing in the woods when Lindsay fights with her? How else could she have handled the situation?

13. What does it mean to be seated with Christ? Is it easy for you to picture it?

14. Do you think God sent the fox to Elita?

15. Elita loves her bedtime routine. What is your bedtime routine?

16. Why do you think it was so hard for Elita to talk to her mom?

17. What did you think about the last scene in the lunchroom when Elita calls other people to come sit with her? Could you imagine doing this in your own school?

18. Which quote do you like more and why? "Every rejection is God's protection," or "All seats provide equal viewing of the universe."

19. Elita learns to pray and read her Bible by the end of the book. What do you think prayer is? What is the Bible, and what makes it different from an ordinary book?

20. How will knowing about being seated with Christ help Elita after middle school? How do you imagine her life after graduating from Siler Middle School?

ACKNOWLEDGMENTS

Thank you to my dad, Brad Brown, for all those nights we sat watching for the red fox in the backyard by Little Hunting Creek and to my mom, Linda Brown, for her advice on helping communicate spiritual truths to children. Thank you for being parents who helped me love nature and for enduring muddy shoes, stitches, and poison ivy. Thank you to my daughters: Sarah for her story of finding her seat with Jesus, and Kate for her wise suggestions as we walked in Park Forest. Thank you to Ashley for endlessly supporting my writing life. As always, thank you to Judy Dunagan, Pam Pugh, and the team at Moody Publishers who first took a chance on an unknown author wanting to write about Ephesians 2:6. I love being seated with Christ alongside you all.

Adventures, friendships, and faith-testers . . . all under the watchful eye of a great big God.

JACK VS. THE TORNADO
978-0-8024-2102-9

THE HUNT FOR FANG
978-0-8024-2103-6

LIONS TO THE RESCUE!
978-0-8024-2104-3

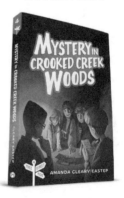

MYSTERY IN CROOKED
CREEK WOODS
978-0-8024-2105-0

MOODY
Publishers®

From the Word to Life®

Discover what it means to be a True Girl after God's own heart.

In this six-week study, you'll enter Ruth's story and learn how you too can become loyal, loving, and godly. True Girl Bible Studies feature important women from Scripture so that, from their examples, we can learn what it looks like to be a True Girl. Each study is designed to help moms lead their daughters in developing a steady love for God's Word.

978-0-8024-2222-4 | also available as an eBook

Miriam's life reminds us that a True Girl practices courageous leadership *right now* because a leader is what she's becoming. Though leaders are imperfect, God offers us second chances to get things right. True Girl Bible Studies help moms and daughters discover how to be women after God's own heart.

978-0-8024-2241-5 | also available as an eBook

MOODY
Publishers®

From the Word to Life®